*Pride Publishing books by S. J. Coles*

**Single Books**
Blood Winter
Straight to the Heart
Dark Summer
The Devil You Know

**Once Upon a Holiday**
Your Christmas
Our Valentine's
My Summer
His Halloween

**Blood and Bonds**
Touch in the Night
Bleed in the Night

**Collections**
My Bloody Valentine: Blood Red Roses
Sun, Sea and Small-Town Secrets
Enemy Territory: My Iron Knight
Secret Santa: Moving Mountains

Blood and Bonds

# BLEED IN THE NIGHT

S. J. COLES

# BLEED IN THE NIGHT

# Dedication

To all the Children of Darkness out there

# Chapter One

Summer was at its height. York hadn't felt a breath of wind or a drop of rain in weeks. Even at night, the air was still and heavy, like it was choked by a storm waiting to break.

But the weather wasn't the reason Tyler couldn't sleep.

It had been the same every night for weeks. As soon as he switched the light off, he was back on Askham Moor. Hands stronger than iron crushed his body. Adrenaline coursed through his veins like venom. The smell of his own urine was sharp in his nostrils.

He could hear his own voice bleeding out of him, freezing and dying in the cold night air: "Let me fucking go," he cried. "Let me go *now*, or I swear I'll..."

The grip on him tightened. Fingernails sharp as glass shards pricked his flesh.

"Be still." The voice was as smooth as an oil spill. It poured into his ear and down his nerves, stretching them to the point of snapping. The hot, fragrant breath against his skin made his traitorous body shake.

"This is assault. I'll have you arrested, I swear."

"This is what happens when weak men pretend they are strong." The creature tightened his grip in Tyler's hair and pulled his head back, exposing his neck. "Do you still think you are strong?"

Tyler fought air into his lungs, staring at the stars that had started to wheel overhead. "Who...who are you?"

"I am Lucien," murmured the voice. "Whether you live another fifty seconds or another fifty years, you will *never* forget that name."

Tyler threw his pillow across the room. It knocked a hi-fi speaker flying. It crashed to the floor with the sickening sound of splintering wood. He sat on the edge of his bed with his head in his hands, breathing hard, until the red mist swirling before his eyes faded.

He checked his phone. Three-o-one a.m. He threw it at the wall, shoved back the sheets and paced the flat until, finally, the sun began to rise, and he dared open the curtains.

By the time he was nearing Fulford Road Police Station an hour later, he was finishing his fourth coffee, and his body felt like it was strung through with hot wire. There was a bitter, metallic taste in his mouth. His heart skittered in his chest.

He swore and swerved to avoid an ambulance bombing the other way down the narrow street...then another. He pulled over and climbed out of the car, shaking as the sirens faded away. Silence descended. He took a steadying breath and made for the police station on foot.

It wasn't yet six a.m., but when he arrived, the entrance was swarming with activity. Another ambulance was pulled up onto the curb. Paramedics were hoisting up a stretcher on which sprawled an unconscious form. There was blood everywhere—on the man's face, clothes, matting his hair. The ambulance screamed off after the others.

Tyler stood staring for a moment before shaking himself and striding into the police station.

"DI Walker," he barked at the harried-looking desk officer. She held up a finger and continued her conversation on the phone. "*Oi*, lady. I said I want to see Walker. *Now*."

"One sec," she said into the phone then gave Tyler a hard look. "Please, sir. Take a seat."

"I won't take a bloody seat. Get Walker out here. *Now*."

The woman's face tightened. "DI Walker is engaged. If you want to leave your number, I will be sure he contacts you. Yes, I'm still here," she spoke again into the phone. "We need extra techs to go over the CCTV as soon as possible. Yes. Scene photographers, too—"

Tyler reached over and cut the woman's call. "I said I want Walker…*now*."

She held his glare without blinking. "And *I* said he's *busy*, sir."

"Mr. Lomax." Tyler turned. A tall man stood in the doorway. His brown hair was disheveled, like he'd been running his hands through it, but the hard amber of his eyes was as unyielding as stone. "You're up early."

"*Finally*," Tyler said, folding his arms. "I came for an update on my case."

The detective studied him for a moment. "This way, Mr. Lomax," he said, stepping back and holding open the door.

Tyler strode through, muttering under his breath. Walker took them to an interview room and shutting them in.

"You're avoiding me," Tyler said.

"Why would I avoid such pleasant company as yours?" Walker replied, standing with his hands in his pockets. There were shadows under his eyes and spots of blood on his collar.

"I'm *serious*," Tyler said, lifting his gaze from the stain. "You don't think I'm serious? Because I can show you just how serious I am, if that's what you want."

"Is that why you're here so early? To threaten me?" Walker replied, pulling out one of the plastic chairs from around the small table and sitting. "Or have you finally come to confess to that assault outside the *Golden Fleece*?"

Tyler bridled. "I'm talking about *my* assault, arsehole. That psycho haemo that attacked me. You know, the one that no one's trying to find?"

"What about the criminal damage to Baron Von Magnusson's home, then?" Walker said coolly. "Perhaps you'd like to confess to that instead?"

"This is *bullshit*. That thing nearly killed me. *Killed* me."

Walker surveyed him a moment longer then gestured to the other chair. "Have a seat, Tyler."

"I won't have a seat. I want to know what you're doing about this."

Walker's only response was to push the chair out from the table with his foot.

Tyler swore and slumped into it, glaring at the detective.

"Are you going to tell me why you're really here this early?"

Tyler's skin rippled at the look in his eyes. "I told you. I wanted an update."

"So you don't know anything about the four men we found on the stairs this morning?"

Tyler blinked. "What?"

"Four unconscious men were dumped in our doorway at shift change, all severely injured. Know anything about that?"

"Why fucking would I?"

Walker interlaced his fingers on the table and leaned forward. "They are two members of a suspected pedophile ring, a violent drug dealer and an abusive husband. Still not ringing any bells?"

Tyler slammed his fist on the table. "I'm here about *Lucien*, Walker. You know, the murderer you've let get away?"

Walker leaned back in this chair again, watching Tyler closely. "Last year the Chief Inspector came for a visit and found a man chained to the railings in the car park. His name was Jason Parr. He was a suspect in a series of rapes. He had a hair band of one of the victims in his pocket. It led to his conviction."

"I'm not here for a history lesson."

"Parr said *you* put him there."

Tyler clenched his fists under the table and was careful not to blink.

"He said you jumped him in a bar," Walker continued, "and next thing he knew he was chained up in the rain with a hairband he claims never to have seen before."

"I don't know no Jason Parr. And that's nothing to do with this."

"So these degenerates left bleeding on our doorstep before dawn…" Walker narrowed his eyes. "Nothing to do with you?"

Tyler stood so suddenly that his chair crashed to the floor. "You better start taking this seriously, detective," he said, stabbing the table with his finger. "Hear me? You don't want a guy like me as your enemy."

He made for the door.

"You want Lucien found, Tyler?" Tyler halted with his hand on the door handle but didn't turn around. "You ask your sister what she knows about this mess," Walker said smoothly. "Then you give me a call."

Tyler glared over his shoulder. "What's she got to do with it?"

"A well-connected woman, your sister," Walker said, standing and straightening his tie. "What she doesn't know isn't worth knowing, right? See what she knows. Then we'll talk."

Tyler stormed out of the police station.

He searched his pockets for his phone, remembered he'd smashed it against his bedroom wall and swore. He got into his car and drove into town with his jaw clenched so hard it hurt. He parked, made for the nearest phone shop and hovered outside the doors until it opened.

The assistant's enthusiasm soon died when he realized that Tyler's money might have no limits but his patience was quite the opposite. He left the store with a new phone and an even worse mood and dialed a number from memory.

Emerald didn't answer.

Tyler fired off a series of furious messages and made for the *Cafe Rouge* on Low Petergate, somewhere that didn't serve alcohol so somewhere he was unlikely to be spotted by anyone he knew. He ordered a black coffee and took a table in the corner, out of the way of the breakfast crowd.

He tried Emerald again with no luck and gulped the scalding coffee. He scrolled several news sites, searching for any mentions of haemophiles. The local papers were still full of articles about the Undying Baron winning the custody case for his adoptive daughter earlier in the year with the help of his human partner, Jesse Truelove. The kid was going to a local school, and Von Magnusson had just been elected to the school board. Reactions were…mixed.

Tyler shook his head, attempting to dispel the memories of standing outside Oswald House, his blood hot with anger, convinced a little girl was being abused behind the high walls.

Then Lucien had turned up.

He quickly switched to the national sites, trying to find anything about any more cases of haemo-on-human violence and what was being done about it. All he found were posts about the haemophile's parliamentary representative Ivor Novák's latest campaign to allow haemophiles to legally marry. Tyler's stomach clenched. He hurriedly scrolled away.

The next thing he found was a video of a press conference around the de-registration of haemophile communes by one Magister Dragomir Soroka. The very sight of the white-faced, white-haired haemophile made Tyler's blood run cold. The eyes, black and empty, reminded him of a shark's.

*Why should our names and addresses be listed for anyone with ill intent to find? Why should we suffer perpetual scrutiny when all we want is a chance to live our lives in peace?*

Tyler put the new phone screen-side down on the table. He finished the coffee. If anything, the caffeine increased his tension, but he ordered a second cup.

By the time he was done with his second drink and Emerald still hadn't returned his call, his patience was frayed to the breaking point. He left the cafe without leaving a tip.

Nasir, Emerald's secretary, started when Tyler strode past his desk.

"Uh, Ty," he said, scurrying after him. "This really isn't a good time."

"Go swivel, Naz," Tyler said and shoved open his sister's office door. He shut it in Nasir's face but not before registering his ex's pained frown.

Emerald was on the phone. Her scarlet suit was as sharp as her gaze, which locked on Tyler and stayed there, even though she didn't miss a beat in her conversation.

"Well, that's exactly what I said. I agree. We just have to get ahead of it. Yes. Exactly. Look…" She tilted her head. "Can I call you back? Ten minutes? Thanks."

She replaced the receiver with a deliberate click. "Tyler. What a nice surprise."

"Leave it out, sis," he said, dropping into one of the armchairs that faced her oversized desk. "If you picked up your bloody phone, I wouldn't have to barge in like this, would I?"

"In case you didn't notice," she said with an icy smile, "the appointment of the lord mayoralty is due.

Getting appointed two years running would make history—and I *intend* to make history. So I have rather a lot on my plate, to say the least."

"I ain't leaving until you talk to me."

Emerald sat motionless with her fingers twined together for such a long time that Tyler knew a sneak of apprehension up his spine. Then she stood, straightened her jacket and went to the door.

Tyler braced himself to be hustled out by security, but instead she just leaned out and said, "Naz?"

"Yes, Lord Mayor?" Nasir scrambled to his feet, tidying papers.

"Take an early lunch. There's a good chap."

Nasir's eyes flicked to Tyler then back. "Yes, Lord Mayor," he said and left.

Emerald waited until the lift doors had pinged shut before closing the door again. She resumed her seat without meeting Tyler's eyes.

"Okay, little brother," she said, leaning back in her seat. "You have four minutes. What do you want?"

"I saw Walker this morning."

She lifted a sculpted eyebrow. "He hasn't taken out a restraining order yet, then." Tyler glowered. "And did the Detective Inspector have any news?"

"You know he didn't. You'd've known before me."

"What's your point Tyler?" she said in a bored tone, doodling on her notepad.

Tyler watched her closely. "Someone dumped four bodies on the steps of the police station overnight."

Emerald stopped doodling. "Excuse me?"

Tyler shook his head. "Not dead. Beat up...bad. There was a lot of fucking blood..."

The sharp lines of her face tightened. "You were there?"

"No," Tyler said hurriedly. "Like I said, I went this morning. They were just clearing up."

"I see." Her expression was watchful.

"Walker asked me if *I* did it. When I put him straight, he asked me to ask *you*."

Emerald had gone very still. "Me?"

Tyler nodded. "Have you heard anything?" Emerald looked at the wall. Tyler dragged his chair closer and lowered his voice. "Please, Emmy. I gotta find that guy. I can't sleep knowing he's out there…"

"And what's your Lucien thing got to do with four scumbags being dumped at Fulford Road?"

Tyler paused. "Who said they were scumbags?" Emerald's red lips twitched. "You know something, Emmy. What is it?"

"Why do you care?"

He swallowed. "Was it Lucien? Did *he* do this?"

Emerald sighed and leaned on her desk. "This didn't come from me. Got it?" Tyler nodded. "I mean it Ty," she said, her voice deadly serious. "If even a whisper of this comes back to me, you can forget about my intervention the next time you get yourself arrested or worse."

"Yeah, yeah," Tyler said, "I get it. I'll take it to the grave. Come on. What's going on, huh?"

Emerald examined her blood-red manicure for a long, tense silence. "Recently people have been… vanishing. Taken out of their homes at night. No signs of a struggle, nothing. They were just…gone. But I got a call this morning. Sounds like they all turned up at the police station—what was left of them, anyway. I wasn't sure I believed it, but you said you saw it?"

"How many went missing?"

"Four, that I've heard of. But it's only become weird because of this last guy...Terry Fleetwood."

"What's so special about him?"

"The other three were under investigation—two for kiddy pictures, another for drugs. Police hadn't been able to get anything solid, probably never would. When they went missing, suspicion was some cop had gone rogue...until Fleetwood vanished."

"Fleetwood was the wife beater?"

"So Walker figured it out, did he?"

"What's the deal with Fleetwood?"

"He *wasn't* under investigation," she said. "Not even suspected. The wife never reported him."

"But *you* knew?"

"I know people who knew," she hedged. "Guy liked to piss away his money in a few of my places, drink and run his mouth, so word got about. But the police were never involved. That means it can't have been a copper that did this."

"So..." He swallowed, his blood running cold. "Lucien?"

She spread her hands. "No one knows. A pro, that was the guess. No struggle, no mess—at least, no mess at the scene of the abductions. No one left behind to care. Though why a pro was targeting these charmers was anyone's guess. But this morning..." Emerald picked up her phone, tapped at the screen and passed it over.

"What's this?" Tyler said, scrolling through some text full of medical terms.

"The medical reports on your gents from this morning."

Tyler scowled. "I don't know what I'm reading here, sis. I failed biology, remember?"

Emerald sighed and took the phone back. "Blood loss, Tyler. They were all suffering from massive blood loss."

Tyler went very still. "Any of them talking?"

"If they are, my source wasn't able to find out."

"So this was him…" Tyler's blood ran cold. "He's still here…in York. *Biting* people. And that moron Walker's doing *nothing* —"

"It's a haemo attack, sure," Emerald said. "Whether it's this Lucien of yours —"

"He's not *mine*," Tyler's face flushed with heat. "He's a fucking maniac. And he's loose in my town, and no one is taking it seriously."

"The city's packed with haemophiles at the moment, Ty," she said, her voice level and infuriatingly calm. "There's a whole contingent of them at Oswald House right now. Blew into town over a month ago. Something to do with this marriage bill Novák is trying to push through with help from that haemo lawyer of the Baron's. Why do you think I'm run off my feet trying to play interference?"

"Lucien attacked these men," Tyler said, stabbing his finger on the desk. "I know it."

"Even if he did, who cares?" she said with a wave of her hand. "Let him clear the scumbags out of the city. Saves me a job."

"You won't be saying that when he starts coming after the scumbags who work for you."

Emerald narrowed her eyes. "Careful."

"Why aren't you up in arms, huh?" he snapped. "Why aren't we all out trying to get this lunatic?"

"Leave it to Walker."

"He's doing fuck-all. Even when he knows all this, I bet —"

"This can't go to the police, Tyler."

Tyler chewed his cheek. "He told me —"

"I have to protect my sources," she said firmly. "We had an agreement."

Tyler made a frustrated noise. "So what am I supposed to do? Nothing?"

"Tyler." Emerald used the voice that always reminded Tyler of their father. "You really have to let this Lucien thing go."

"*Why*?"

"Because you can't hurt him, but he could hurt you...*really* hurt you."

Tyler again felt the hot breath on his neck, the hands crushing his body. He heard the voice like liquid mercury flowing through him, lighting fires as it went.

"If no one else will stop this guy," he said, his voice hoarse, "then I'll bloody have to do it myself."

"Tyler," Emerald said, glancing at her phone as it started ringing, "do as I say. Let it go. Take a holiday or something."

"A *holiday*?"

"Get out of town for a while. When was the last time you went anywhere, huh?" She reached for the phone.

Tyler grabbed the phone before she could answer it, lifted the receiver and slammed it back down. Emerald's eyes glinted with dark fire.

"What else do you have?" he said. "Anything you've heard — rumors, anything."

She was silent for a moment then tilted her head. "What about Naz, huh?" she asked, frowning. "What went wrong there?"

"Emerald —"

"You need something, Ty," she went on. "If it's not headspace, then it's to get laid."

"Tell me what you know about Lucien."

Emerald sighed loudly. "This isn't like knocking some creep's head on the bar and tying him to a railing, little brother. Haemophiles are dangerous. You're lucky to be alive as it is."

Tyler ground his teeth. "Well, I guess I'll have to fight fire with fire."

"What?"

"I need one of *them*. A haemo."

"Ty, no—"

"If you won't help me, I'll bloody well help myself," he said and stormed out, just as her phone started ringing again. He passed Nasir on the bridge outside the office. He was carrying a takeaway coffee and a paper bag that smelled of pastry. His face transformed as he saw Tyler approach, but Tyler brushed past him without meeting his eyes.

\* \* \* \*

Despite the A/C in his car, by the time he reached Oswald House, his blood was burning hotter than ever. The events of the morning rolled in his head like rocks in a landslide. The sun beat down out of a merciless, clear sky. But under it all, ever-present, unrelenting, was the ice-encrusted layer of fear that had formed inside him the moment Lucien had laid hands on him.

He swore to himself, pulled in at the locked gate, wound down his window, put his thumb on the buzzer and held it there. The cameras over the gate whirred and tilted toward his car. He buzzed again.

"Answer, for Christ's sake."

There was a crackle, and a voice came on the line. "Can we help you, sir?"

"You can let me in."

"Do you have an appointment?"

"Tell your boss it's Tyler Lomax. He will want to see me if he knows what's good for him."

A long silence. Then again, that crackle. "I'm sorry, Mr. Lomax. You are not on the appointment list, and the Baron is not currently available."

"Let me in this second, or I swear — "

"Sir," the voice said firmly, "we are requesting you leave the premises immediately or we will summon the authorities."

Tyler swore, slammed out of his car and scrambled over the wall. He strode up the drive toward the mansion with his face burning. The building was large. Its white walls shone achingly bright in the hot sunshine. All the blinds were drawn, and it was oddly still and quiet. He shook away unease then slowed when two security guards moved to intercept him.

"Let's not have a scene sir," one of them said, gesturing back toward the gate.

"You might wanna get outta my way."

"You are trespassing," the other guard said. "Leave now, and we won't press charges."

"Fuck you," Tyler said and moved shoulder past them, but the men grabbed him, spun him around and began to march him to the gate. He swore and struggled, shouting obscenities.

"Hold it," called a voice from behind them.

The men turned. Tyler stilled. His emotion hardened into a kernel of angry surprise.

Jesse Truelove was striding toward them. He had his hands in the pockets of a pair of denim cut-offs that were slung tantalizingly low on his slim hips. He wore a tight black T-shirt that clung to his sculpted torso and left his tattooed arms bare. His messy black hair fell in his eyes and his pierced lip and eyebrow were twisted in the glare of the sun.

Tyler was catapulted back to the Evil Eye cocktail lounge, to the night he'd spotted Jesse across the crowded room—the hot need he'd read in Jesse's face that had gone right to his dick.

When Jesse had started to feature in the news reports around the Baron's adoption, not to mention Trixy Jazz's viral haemophile sex-lives documentary, Tyler had found it harder and harder to forget their hot and heavy fuck against Jesse's kitchen counter.

It had been the last time Tyler had had sex and actually enjoyed it. But the memory of Jesse dismissing him the second they were done still stung like a fresh sunburn.

"You."

Jesse gave him a look that made Tyler fume and grow horny at the same time. The guy was just too attractive to be legal—and now he was fucking a haemophile. Tyler clenched his teeth.

"What do you want, Tyler?"

"I want these tossers to get their hands off me."

Jesse's eyes filled with scorn, but he nodded to the security guys. "Let him go. He'll only come back if we chuck him out like a bad penny." The security guards reluctantly let him go and moved off at a nod from Jesse. "There," he said. "That it?"

"No, it's not bloody *it*," Tyler growled. "I want a fucking word, don't I?"

Jesse sighed, turned on his heel and made for the house. "Come on then. But you better make it quick."

# Chapter Two

The interior of Oswald House was dim and cool, a stark contrast to the heat and brightness of outside. But as Jesse led Tyler through the marble hall to an airy sitting room, Tyler's blood still burned in his veins.

Jesse dropped himself on one of the deep sofas. "Okay, Tyler. What do you want?"

"I wanna speak to your boss—or is he your boyfriend now?"

"Fiancé, actually," Jesse said, lifting his left hand where a platinum band shone on his fourth finger.

Tyler curled his lip. "You're kidding."

"Why? Jealous?"

Tyler's face heated. "Like hell. Figures it would take a freak of nature to wanna marry someone like you."

"Dad?" A small voice came from behind them. Tyler started and turned. A little girl stood in the doorway. She had big, blue eyes and blonde ringlets the color of sunshine. She clutched a large artist's tablet to her chest and was staring at Tyler with wide, wary eyes. Jesse was on his feet in an instant.

"Hey, Dim, love," he said, hurrying to the door and crouching down next to her. "You okay?"

She nodded, her uncertain eyes still locked on Tyler. Her gaze was firing discomfort through his nerves like electricity, but he couldn't look away. "I just wanted to show you my new picture."

"I'd love that," Jesse said softly, with a warm smile on his face that smoothed away all the pinched sharpness he had directed at Tyler. "But I'm just talking to this man right now. Head back up to your room. I'll be up there in a couple of minutes."

"Promise?"

Jesse ruffled her hair. "Promise. Off you go."

She left, and Jesse shut the door and folded his arms. Anger hardened his green eyes to bottle glass. "You were saying? About my family being freaks?"

Tyler shifted uncomfortably but didn't break eye contact. "I wanna talk to him…the Baron…now."

"It's daytime, you moron. He's asleep."

Tyler felt a rush of raw, sickening embarrassment and clenched his fists. "Later then. I'll fucking wait."

"You're lucky I've let you in for five minutes, let alone five hours."

"There's a goddamn killer on the loose," Tyler snapped. "The psycho haemo that attacked me here. Now he's attacking people in town."

Jesse's face turned grim. "What?"

"Four guys were dumped outside the police station last night, bled almost dry. Police aren't doing anything. And it's your fucking 'fiancé's' mate that's doing it."

"They're not 'mates', Tyler."

"Like hell they aren't. I saw the way they looked at each other. I heard what they said."

"Was that before or after you pissed your pants?"

Tyler's rage flattened to ice in his gut. He stepped close and lowered his voice. "I'm going to find this Lucien guy. And I can remember you and your tame vampire either helped—or you didn't."

Jesse raised an eyebrow. "We're not scared of you, Tyler Lomax."

Tyler refused to look away, even though Jesse's eyes were making his skin tingly. "The Baron depends on my sister's goodwill for a lot of business in this town. People are just starting to get over the whole adoption thing." Tyler looked him hard in the eyes. "It would be a real shame if life got difficult for him again, just as the little girl was getting settled."

Jesse's eyes swam with a mixture of fury and fear. The fury won. "Piss off," he said, yanking the door open. "Piss off and get a life."

Tyler ground his teeth. "You're an idiot, Jesse Truelove," Tyler said in a low voice. "A loser and a coward, too. If your boyfriend had any balls, he'd be out hunting for this psycho already."

"You shouldn't talk about what you don't understand," Jesse said.

"You're a coward," Tyler repeated. "Letting everyone else clear up your mess. And God help you if I ever see you around town again."

Tyler stormed away before Jesse could respond.

The gate was open. The security men stood watching through their sunglasses as he returned to his car. He muttered to himself as he backed out into the country lane, then gunned off back toward town, just as his phone started buzzing.

The Bluetooth display in his dashboard said *Brandon Calling…*

Tyler answered by pushing a command on his steering wheel.

"What?"

A startled pause. "Jesus, Ty. Nice to speak to you, too."

"What do you want?"

"Word is you went down to Fulford Road this morning. That Walker got any news or what?"

"Don't you think I'd've called you if he had?"

"I dunno, Ty. Don't know who you talk to these days. Not seen hide nor hair of you down at the pub for weeks."

"Perhaps I don't feel like pissing about in the pub with you lot," he said, gripping his wheel tighter as the anger sharpened in his gut.

Brandon made a disparaging noise. "Still not sleeping, huh?"

Tyler muttered under his breath, steering down the winding lanes, trying to wrestle his raging thoughts into order.

"Look… Where are you?"

"Why?" Tyler muttered.

"I'm outside your place. Been calling all morning."

"Well, I'm not there, clearly."

"Smart ass. Just meet me at the Guy Fawkes Inn, okay?"

Brandon hung up. Tyler checked his watch. It was after noon. *Definitely time for a beer.*

Brandon was in the farthest corner of the pub's beer garden, on a table screened from the rest by some planters and fencing. His bull-necked form was crushed into a mustard polo shirt, his eyes were bleary, likely with a hangover, and there was sunburn across his receding hairline. He gave Tyler a nod as he joined him, but the first thing Tyler did was to lift the pint of ice-cold lager that was waiting for him and swallow half in one go.

"Rough morning?" Brandon asked.

Tyler lowered the pint and breathed deep, rubbing his eyes. "What did you want, Brandon?"

"Wanted to know what Walker said," Brandon muttered, sipping his own drink and scowling, his heavy-browed face twisting.

"I told you…nothing," Tyler muttered. "Now this thing's attacking people in their homes, and everyone is still just giving me the bloody run-around."

Brandon planted his meaty elbows on the table and leaned close. "No one's going to do nothing neither, Ty—not while all the lefties are up in arms trying to let them get married and shit."

Tyler drank more beer and glared at the tabletop. "I'm working on it," he muttered. "I just don't know where to bloody start."

"I got somewhere you can start."

Tyler looked up, frowning. His friend's face was shining with sweat, but his eyes were cold. He pushed a scrap of paper across the table. Tyler took it. A phone number was scrawled across it in blue ink.

"What's this?"

"The cavalry."

"Huh?"

Brandon twisted his mouth in a grimace. "I told you there are people out there that deal with this sort of thing," Brandon murmured. "Specialists."

Tyler stared at the paper. "This is what I think it is?"

Brandon nodded. "Took me a while to get it. They don't give their numbers out to just anyone. But I told them we were there, on the moor that night. Told them what that bastard did to you."

A shiver went through Tyler, despite the close heat of the crowded beer garden. "I said I wanted to deal with this myself."

"And it's been months and you've got nowhere," Brandon insisted. "I was there, too, Tyler. I saw the murder in them glowing eyes. He'd've ripped your head off, given half a chance."

"I bloody know that, don't I?"

"It fucked us *both* up, you know," Brandon said in a harsh whisper. "We're both on edge, jumping at shadows. Well, I'm fucking sick of it. Something needs to be done about this freak of nature running loose in our city. Who knows who he'll go after next? Maybe he'll come back to finish the job, even." Brandon glared. "If you don't call that number, I will."

Tyler stared at the paper. "I dunno, Brandon," he said carefully. "I'm all for getting something done…but I've heard some nasty shit about these types."

"This is already nasty shit," Brandon said. "Time to fight fire with fire."

Tyler rubbed his mouth. His head ached. His stomach rolled with the beer.

"Time to draw a line in the sand," Brandon said in a low, dangerous voice. "Time to show these bastards you can't just walk into our town, start kidnapping kids and attacking people in their homes. Where's it gonna end, huh?"

Tyler recognized the fierce light in his friend's eyes. Brandon really was scared. Seeing his own emotion mirrored so deeply in another's face sent a shock of electricity through his body. He crumpled the number into his pocket, downed his beer and stood.

"Call the number, Tyler," Brandon called after him. "Make this right."

Tyler left the pub with his head spinning. The city was choked with tourists. He wove among the crowds, not registering the press of bodies or the noise. He crossed the river and kept going, striding along the hot pavements, trying to get a handle on his thoughts, the paper in his pocket heavy as lead.

By the time the sun was starting to set, he was miles from home and his stomach was reminding him that he hadn't eaten all day, but he was still no closer to figuring out what to do. He sat on a bench overlooking the river, pulled out the crumpled paper and his phone. He stared at both as the sky darkened.

With a rush like nausea, he found he'd dialed the number. It rang...and rang. No one answered. It rang out and went dead. Tyler let out a breath, the sense of anticlimax hollow and pained. He chewed his lip, staring at his phone and contemplating trying again, when a text message pinged in.

*Ye Olde Starre Inn. One hour.*

Tyler blinked at it, then stood, his limbs like stone. He checked his watch then turned along the river back toward town. His pace quickened as the sun sank below the horizon and night rolled in.

He was glad to get back to the bustle and lit streets of the city center.

He took a table in an empty snug in the Ye Olde Starre Inn, ordered steak and chips and drank two pints while he waited. His food arrived. The hour came and went. Nothing happened.

He pushed his half-eaten food away, ran his hand over his short-cropped hair and stared at the ceiling. He got another pint. He'd finished that and was making inroads into his fourth when a slim figure slid into the booth opposite him.

Tyler blinked. For an instant he was sure the person sitting opposite him couldn't possibly be real. He had a mop of curly black hair, skin a practically edible shade of caramel and eyes such a pale gray they shone like silver. His wide, white smile had a devilish tilt—and that, combined with his slanting eyebrows, gave him a boyish, elfin appearance that was almost too beautiful to be human.

Tyler stared dumbly, and the man's smile twitched.

"Mr. Lomax?" His voice was sweet, lilting with the hint of an accent Tyler in his befuddled state couldn't identify.

"Who the fuck are you?"

"Potentially your new best friend."

"Oh yeah?" Tyler said, downing another large mouthful of beer. "How's that?"

"You tell me. You called me."

Tyler blinked. "You're the one that sent that text?"

The man scanned the room, but the other patrons were all absorbed in their own meals and drinks. He put his elbows on the table and leaned close. A dark curl fell into his eyes, and Tyler detected a soft, earthy scent, like tree bark and sunshine on leaves.

"I hear you wanna catch a vampire?"

Tyler stared at him. When he spoke, his voice was hoarse. "Come again?"

"There's a nasty piece of work out there right now," the man continued. "He attacked you and is now attacking others. The police can't stop him. The haemos don't want to stop him. So you've decided to take matters into your own hands, right?"

"How do you know all this?"

The man's smile tilted, dimpling his cheek. "You're not exactly low-profile around here, Mr. Lomax. Neither is what happened to you."

Tyler narrowed his eyes. "Okay. So where do you fit in?"

"Call me a...specialist." The man spread his hands. He had very long, slim fingers and wide palms. "At your service."

Tyler leaned in closer, examining him narrowly though the blur of alcohol. "And who in the hell are you, exactly?"

"You can call me Damon," he said and held out one of those long, pretty hands. "Perhaps I could call you Tyler?"

Tyler looked at the hand then at the bewitching face without moving. "Let's not get ahead of ourselves," he murmured. "First of all, tell me what exactly you can do."

Damon moved around the table closer to Tyler. Tyler's blood spiked when he caught sight of skin-tight jeans hugging the man's long, slim legs. He held himself rigid as Damon's arm brushed his.

"I want the same things you want, Tyler — safe streets, the ability to sleep soundly without worrying what might be lurking in the dark."

Tyler swallowed. "So, what? You're some kind of...vampire hunter?"

Damon laughed, a free, vibrant sound that had Tyler's sluggish blood pumping hard. "That sounds very *Buffy the Vampire Slayer*." His grin was playful.

"Let's just say I have some…unique skills. Skills that could be used to your advantage."

"I want Lucien," Tyler said, the words sounding loaded, even to himself.

"Now we're talking plainly." Damon smiled again. "Tell me what you know."

"I know he attacked four men and dumped them at the police station last night," Tyler muttered. "I know he's out of control — that it's only a matter of time before he kills someone, if he hasn't already."

Damon regarded him levelly. "The Fulford Road incident. I heard about it. And you think it was Lucien?"

"The detective in charge as much as told me so. He didn't have anything to go on. Told me to talk to my sister…Emerald Lomax." Damon's eyes glinted but he didn't speak. "She knew who the victims were and the fact that whoever attacked them knew they were scumbags, even when the police didn't, and got them out of their homes without a struggle or leaving any trace."

"Good. This is a good start. So, here's the deal." Damon lay one of his long-fingered hands flat on the table close to Tyler's. "I can help you find the haemophile known as Lucien. I can even help you catch the toothy fucker…for a price."

"How much are we talking?"

"Here," Damon said, sliding a business card over the table. "Throw away that other number. That's what we call the central line. This is how you can reach me directly. My fee is on the back. Think about it if you want, but I promise" — Damon stood and hooked his thumbs in his belt and grinned — "I take client satisfaction very seriously."

The hairs on Tyler's neck prickled. He lowered his gaze to the business card and turned it over. He bridled at the figure scrawled there. But when he looked up to protest, Damon had vanished.

* * * *

That night, once again, Tyler lay on his bed, wakeful, staring at the ceiling. That voice again echoed in his head.

*"I am Lucien. Whether you live another fifty seconds or another fifty years, you will never forget that name."*

At four a.m., he gave up, got out of bed and went to make coffee.

He was on his third cup and was squinting at some reality TV show on his seventy-five-inch TV when his doorbell jerked him out of his stupor.

The doorbell app on his phone showed a handsome young man standing in the hall with a work bag over one shoulder and a nervous look on his face.

Tyler scowled and pressed the voice button. "Piss off, Naz."

"I just want to talk, Tyler. Please? You owe me that much."

Tyler sighed and slunk to the front door to open it. He returned to the living room and dropped back onto the sofa. Nasir hovered in the doorway, looking him up and down.

"You look like shit, just for the record."

"Nice talk," Tyler grumbled and swallowed the last of his cooling coffee.

Nasir looked around at the dirty mugs and plates then the coffee table crowded with takeaway cartons.

"Well?" Tyler said, flicking through the channels. "Are you going to talk or just give my place the stink-eye?"

Nasir grabbed the remote from him and turned the TV off. "I want to know what's going on with you."

"A couple of shags and suddenly you're my childminder?"

Nasir's face colored but he didn't move. "I thought we were mates. We used to be, at least. And I know you don't have many left. So, tell me. When was the last time you actually slept the night through?"

"None of your business," Tyler said, rubbing his face. "Or Emmy's, if she's the one that sent you."

"She didn't send me," Nasir said and perched on the edge of the armchair. "You realize this obsession of yours has become unhealthy, right?"

"*Obsession*?"

"Come on, Tyler."

"That freak *attacked* me," Tyler said, low and level. "It could come back any night to finish me off. And no one fucking cares."

"That's not true—"

"Police have fuck all. Emmy won't help them. No one freaking *cares*—"

"You don't know what the police have," Nasir said calmly. "And there are seven haemophiles staying at Oswald House right now, Ty. Seven."

Tyler blinked blearily. "So the Baron's got his mates over. So what?"

Nasir gave him a level look. "Did you not consider that they might be here to deal with Lucien? And that they are probably the best people to do the job?"

Tyler blinked, his skin prickling. "You don't know that."

"No, I don't. But they have to register when they are in the area. I know they are staying indefinitely. Oswald House isn't a commune. Why else would they be here?"

"They don't care what Lucien does."

"You don't know that."

"Yes, I do," Tyler insisted. "I went up there yesterday...to Oswald House."

Nasir frowned. "Why?"

"I wanted some accountability," Tyler snapped. "And maybe I thought what you thought, that Von Magnusson should clean up his own mess. But they blew me off."

"They're trying to integrate," Nasir said reasonably. "Individuals like Lucien give them a bad name. That's not in anyone's best interest. But they're not gonna publicize what they plan to do about it. They don't want things to seem worse than they already are."

Tyler plucked at the sofa cushion. "So what will they do if they catch him?"

"They're supposed to hand him over to the authorities. But we've all heard of haemos settling their own matters internally. He'd likely just...vanish. We'd never know what happened."

Tyler suddenly felt sick and couldn't explain why. "I don't care," he said, standing and sweeping into the kitchen. "Whatever they're doing, they're not doing it fast enough."

"Have you stopped to ask yourself what this is really all about, Ty?" Nasir said, leaning in the kitchen doorway.

"What?"

"I know you're not really this guy," he said gently. "All this attitude and lashing out? This is fear talking."

"What the fuck do you know?"

"I know you used to have fun. Go out. Have a laugh. You had principles, sure, but you weren't a dick about it. And I'll tell you this for free. Living off your inheritance was more attractive when you didn't just throw your weight about and piss vinegar all over the place."

"What am I supposed to do?" Tyler snapped, slamming his mug on the counter. "Pretend everything was normal when I almost got killed?"

"No, of course not," Nasir said, frowning. "But this isn't that kind of fear, is it?"

Tyler drank a glass of water and slammed the glass down. "You don't know what you're talking about."

Nasir stepped close. Tyler could smell his musky cologne and clean clothes. He gripped the glass tight. "I know you well enough to tell when you're ashamed and trying to hide it."

"*Excuse* me?"

"People have got up in your face before," Nasir said smoothly, heading for the door. "You set them straight and got on with your life...every time." He paused in the doorway and gave him a level look. "I guarantee if you admit why you're really obsessed with this Lucien character, you'll be able to sleep."

Heat rode through Tyler. "Leave, Naz. *Now*."

Nasir returned to the living room to collect his bag. He paused in the doorway to give Tyler a long, assessing look. "There has to be a reason you didn't want to touch me, Tyler," he said. "Why you didn't want *me* touching *you*? There's a reason you only wanted to watch."

"Naz...*go*."

Nasir did as he was told. The silence in the flat after he'd closed the door was suffocating.

Tyler swore and pulled out his phone.

It rang only once before a pleasantly accented voice answered. "Mr. Lomax. You're up early."

"Let's do this," Tyler grated. "I want this son of a bitch out of my life…yesterday."

A pause. "And my fee?"

"Anything," Tyler said. "I'll give you anything you want. Just get this done."

"You've got yourself a deal," Damon said, and Tyler could hear the smile in his voice. "Be in tonight. I'll be in touch."

Tyler was restless all day. He half-heartedly tidied, the look on Nasir's face still fresh in his memory, loading the dishwasher and throwing all his dirty clothes in the machine. He ordered a curry and ate it in front of the TV, drinking beer and making himself concentrate on some cop show with about twelve different storylines. His eyelids grew heavy. Exhaustion sucked at him like the pull of a tide. He checked his watch. Still hours before Damon was due to contact him.

He had time to rest his eyes, just for a minute…

\* \* \* \*

"Why are you hunting me?"

Tyler sat up with a curse. Night had fallen. The only light in the room was from the TV. Tyler scanned the shadows, his heart pounding.

"I asked you a question."

Tyler spun around. A dark figure stood outlined against the window. It was lean, in a long coat, despite the warm night. Sleek, dark hair caught the streetlight bleeding in the window. The face was completely in shadow.

"How did you get in here?" Tyler's voice shook.

"Why are you hunting me, Tyler?" the figure repeated. The voice was as smooth and dark as the space between the stars.

"You're gonna pay," Tyler growled, finally finding the strength to stand. "Gonna get you for what you did to me."

The figure drifted forward. The feet made no noise on the laminate floor. It stepped into the light. It glowed on sharp cheekbones, curving lips and a pair of crimson eyes fringed in thick lashes. The flame-hot gaze pinned Tyler to the spot. Lucien came close enough for Tyler to feel his breath on his chin. His head filled with a faint but dizzying scent, copper mixed with hot wine, so distinct he could almost swallow it.

"I was protecting my family." Tyler had to watch keenly to actually see his lips move. It was like he was talking right into his mind. "I would have gone further, but you are misguided rather than evil. I had chosen to forget you…but you insist on not being forgotten."

"You attacked those guys," Tyler said, his voice shaking worse than ever. "The ones from the police station. You bit them. Drank them dry."

"I could have done much worse. They will at least live to face the consequences of their actions."

"Yeah? Well, so will you."

Lucien leaned in and inhaled. His eyes fluttered closed. Tyler's blood chilled in his veins. His jaw ached with clenching. His body tingled, still frozen, refusing to obey.

"You're not scared of me, Tyler Lomax," Lucien said, opening his glowing eyes. "Why do you pretend you are?"

"You better fucking kill me," Tyler grated between clenched teeth. "And do it now. 'Cause I'm coming after you, I swear."

The blood-colored gaze held Tyler to the spot for another breathless moment. Tyler could have brushed the hair behind his ears if he'd wanted. His fingers pulsed at the thought.

"Let it go, Tyler," Lucien whispered. "This will be your only warning."

The ring of the doorbell made Tyler jump. He stood, blinking around the dark living room. He was alone. His head was fuzzy and his mouth dry. He hurried to the windows and checked them all, but they were all closed and locked. He rubbed his eyes.

"A dream," he said to himself, willing himself to believe it, even though he knew better. "Just another fucking dream."

The doorbell rang again. He checked his phone. It was Damon.

Tyler turned on every light in the flat and opened the door.

"Good evening," Damon said but then his smile dropped as he took in the look on Tyler's face. "Everything okay?"

"Course," Tyler said, stepping back and opening the door wider. "So, are we on?"

"Oh, we are on, my friend," Damon said as he moved through into the living room. Tyler watched the way he moved, sinuous as a snake, with something like interest fizzing in his blood. He tried to blame the supposed dream, just like he had tried to blame the booze the day before. But no, he had to admit now…this guy, whoever he was, was sexy as hell and knew it. "Nice place you have here," he said with a knowing half-smile that went straight to Tyler's groin.

"Drink?" he said, moving hastily into the kitchen.

"Sure. What you got?"

"Anything," Tyler said, opening the drinks cabinet. "Beer. Wine. Whiskey. Vodka."

"A connoisseur I see," Damon said, leaning close and examining the line of spirits with another. "However, it's been very hot again today. A cold beer would hit the spot more than anything."

Tyler retrieved two bottles from the back of the fridge and opened them with the ring set into the wall. Damon took his drink and tilted it toward Tyler.

"To a fruitful partnership."

Tyler clinked his bottle without meeting the guy's eyes then drank. Damon took a deep swallow and Tyler watched, half-dazed, as his neck muscles moved then dropped his gaze.

"So, where do we start?"

"The living room?" Damon said with a suggestive smile.

"I didn't mean..." Tyler said, avoiding the silver gaze once more. "What do we start *with*?"

Damon chuckled. He moved through to the living room, and he set his bag on the armchair Nasir had sat in earlier that day.

Tyler shook his head. That visit already felt like a week ago. He made himself not look at the spot by the window where Lucien had appeared in his supposed dream...

"I've already started." Damon pulled four cardboard files out of his backpack and put them on the coffee table.

"What are those?"

"The police files on your friends from the station."

"How did you get them?" he said, sitting and opening the file on top.

"I told you. I'm a professional," Damon said with that glint back in his eye.

Tyler stared at the mugshot in the first file — an aging guy with a craggy face and a bleary, oyster-pale gaze.

"Donald Bramstone." Damon curled his lip. "Under investigation for distributing child pornography. A real gentleman."

Tyler turned the page and froze. He was staring at a series of photos of Bramstone, withered and pale in a hospital bed, his head tilted to one side to reveal the jagged wound in his neck. The next photo was a close-up of the wound, deep and inflamed, red with fresh bleeding.

"This is…a bite?" Tyler murmured softly.

"It's a bite all right," Damon said flatly. "Lucien left him just enough juice to confess to his crimes in the ambulance. Next, we have Craig Dennings," Damon went on, opening the next file to reveal a picture of a smart-dressed man with a suit, a suntan and salt-and-pepper hair. "An associate of our friend Bramstone. His accountant, if you can believe it. I believe business was booming, too." Another wry scowl as he opened the third file to a picture of a washed-out looking man with brown, cracked teeth. "Klaus Mussen, some small-time drug dealer. Beat up some kid when he came up short for his weekly score of hash. And, finally," Damon opened the last file to the photo of a younger man with messy brown hair and a narrow, sullen gaze. "Terry Fleetwood. Petty theft, drunk and disorderly and, more recently" — Damon's eyes were flat and hard — "domestic abuse. So, recognize any of them?"

"Just this wanker," Tyler said, tapping Fleetwood's photo. "Saw him getting loaded into the ambulance."

"You didn't know him already?" Tyler shook his head. Damon lifted Tyler's TV remote. "You mind?"

Tyler shrugged.

Damon turned the TV on, linked his phone to the screen and brought up a map of York. There were four red pins set at different points around the city. "This is where they all lived. As you can see, nowhere near each other. So, it's not likely they attended the same dance class or anything like that."

"How does this get us to Lucien?"

"I'm trying to find out how *he* found *them*," Damon said levelly, tapping the files. "If we find the pattern, we find the haemo. Come on, boyo. You're a local lad. What do you know about these guys? What have they all got in common besides douchebaggery?"

"Nothing that I can see... Wait..." He stood and approached the TV. "Zoom in here." Damon obeyed, enlarging the view of a street to the south of town with a single red pin. Tyler scowled at the screen. "This is Fleetwood's place?"

"You know it?"

"It's one of mine," Tyler murmured, skimming through Fleetwood's file. "One of our rental properties."

"Really?" Damon said, doubtful.

Tyler gave him a look. "Emerald and I, we've got some places...off the books, so we can rent them cheap for those who need it."

Damon raised an eyebrow. "How philanthropic."

Tyler turned another page and stared at a photo of a woman. She had her top rolled up to reveal bruising across her ribs. She was looking steadfastly away from the camera, but he recognized her hard, blue eyes.

Damon eyed him. "You know her?"

Tyler nodded. "Charlene Tibbs. I got her the house. I knew she got married... Kinda lost touch after that. Never knew who her fella was." The file started to shake in Tyler's hands. "That fucking arsehole."

"You think she'll talk to you?"

"Won't the police have already done that?"

"She might tell you things she wouldn't tell them. Right?"

"Sure. Maybe."

"Great. We'll go tomorrow." He drained his beer and gathered the files, then tucked them into his bag. "We're making progress, my friend. You should be pleased." His grin turned feral. "Am I performing as well as you hoped?"

Tyler stared at his tilting lips then at his long-fingered hands grasping his hips. His blood stirred. Something shifted in Damon's eyes.

"We could do something other than shake on this...if you want."

Tyler swallowed. Blood pooled in his groin at the thought. But he took a step back. "This is strictly business, mate."

"If that's what you want. But, just for the record, I'm not opposed to mixing work with pleasure." Damon's teeth flashed. Tyler swallowed as Damon studied him closely then looked away. "Another time maybe. Rest up, big guy..." He moved to the door. "Big day tomorrow."

Tyler didn't even try going to bed. His nerves were strung too tight, and that dream still felt too close to the surface. He moved around the flat, checking window and door locks, then watched some made-for-TV movie that had his head pounding with boredom. He tried some porn next, some of his favorite stuff from his private collection, all gorgeous boys with oil, toys and bodies straight from his wildest dreams. But no matter how much he grasped and pumped his cock, he couldn't get hard.

\* \* \* \*

"Didn't sleep, huh?" Damon asked with a sideways glance as Tyler drove them to Charlene's the next morning.

"What are you, my doctor?"

Damon fell silent. Tyler sipped his double-strength coffee and attempted to blink the bleariness from his eyes.

There was a beat-up two-door hatchback in the drive of Charlene's house and a rusted garden bench on the lawn, but otherwise the house was tidy and well kept, especially compared to the rest of the houses on the street. Charlene opened the door only after Tyler had rung the bell a third time. Her deep frown melted into surprise.

"Fuck. Tyler?"

"Hey, Charlene. How's things?"

She glanced warily at Damon then back again. "Been better, if I'm honest. What do you want? Not behind on rent, am I?"

"No. Nothing like that."

"Can we come in, Mrs. Fleetwood?" Damon asked.

"It's Miss Tibbs now, actually," Charlene said with a sharp look. "And who are you?"

"He's a mate," Tyler said gently. "Nothing funny, Charlene. We just want a word, that's all."

She looked at them both doubtfully for another long moment then opened the door. They moved through into the open-plan kitchen and living room. There were boxes on the floor, piled with broken picture frames, DVDs, CDs and men's clothes.

"See anything you want, take it," she said as she moved into the kitchen and put the kettle on. "The rest is getting burnt."

"Shit, Charlene," Tyler said, eyeing a torn-up wedding photograph in the nearest box. "Why didn't you tell me, huh?"

She gave him a defiant look. "What do you know, exactly?"

"That your husband is an arsehole."

"*Ex*-husband," she insisted, getting mugs out of the cupboard. "Solicitor's getting me a deal on the court fees. We'll be divorced before his sorry arse gets out of jail — *if* it gets out, that is."

"Glad to hear it, ma'am," Damon said, scanning the room with his silvery eyes.

"Who is this again, Ty?" Charlene snapped.

"Told you, a mate."

Charlene examined Damon narrowly. "Always did manage to snag the pretty ones." She said with a tight smile. "You'll have to share your secret."

Damon raised his eyebrows, and Tyler clenched his teeth. "We're just working together."

"Working on what?"

Tyler looked at Damon who gave him an infinitesimal nod. "We're after the guy that got Terry."

Her face hardened. "Come again?"

"He was attacked, right?" Tyler said, stepping closer to her. "Nearly killed."

"So the police said. But I don't know nothing about whoever did it, apart from the fact that I'd like to buy them a pint. You want tea or coffee?"

"Coffee," Tyler said.

Damon waved a hand. "Just water for me, please."

She spooned instant coffee into a mug and poured on the boiled water before getting a pint glass to fill with tap water.

"What happened to Terry, Miss Tibbs? Do you know?"

"He went out on the piss and didn't come back," Charlene said, handing the drinks over and returning to the kitchen to make tea for herself. She suddenly looked very tired. "Wasn't the first time. Wasn't the first time I'd been grateful for it, too. But I assumed he was passed out on someone's couch somewhere until the coppers banged on my door. And frankly, I'm not interested in knowing more. He was asking for trouble. He got it. End of story." She narrowed her eyes. "Why do you care, anyway?"

"Whoever attacked Terry," Tyler said quietly, "wasn't anyone human, Charlene."

Charlene's eyes darkened. "What?"

"It was a haemophile. The same one that attacked me."

Charlene started for a long time. "Okay," she eventually said. "I get it now. 'Cause I wouldn't want you going after anyone on my account. Whoever did this, he's done me a favor."

"Again, why didn't you tell *me* about all this?" Tyler said, setting the coffee aside.

"'Cause I knew what you'd do, Tyler Lomax. This vamp's gone easy on Terry compared to what you would have done."

"So? It's like you said, he had it coming…and more. I could have sorted him out years ago, if you'd said something."

"I *loved* him, you moron."

Tyler snorted in disbelief. "You expect me to believe that?"

Charlene narrowed her eyes. "Come back and say that when you love someone you shouldn't, someone you live and breathe for, even though you're risking body and soul to be with them. *Then* you can judge."

Tyler's skin chilled, despite the stuffiness of the room. He felt Damon's eyes on him.

"Is there anything else you can tell us, Miss Tibbs?" Damon said. "Any recent changes to his routine or new people in his life?"

Charlene stared at the floor. "Terry hasn't even changed a pair of socks since we got together. He worked. He drank. He hit me. That was it." She raised her eyes. "I wasn't ready to admit what he was for a long time, Tyler—to myself, let alone to anyone else. Whoever this was took the choice out of my hands." She shrugged. "It's like the universe knew I'd reached my limit. I was this close to knifing the guy myself." She sipped her tea.

"Thank you for your time," Damon said after silence had stretched on for several moments. He set his glass down. "Best of luck."

Tyler opened his mouth to continue to argue then paused, noticing Damon's glass for the first time. It had a pub logo etched into the side.

"Wait," Tyler said, lifting the glass. "Did Terry Drink in the Dunnington Arms?"

"Yeah," she smiled. "It's where we met. Still got Happy Hour on a Friday. Remember the lock-ins?" She shook her head, and her smile turned sad. "Would be nice to go back, wouldn't it? To when we didn't have to be so grown up about everything?"

Tyler set the glass down. "We'll cut your rent, Charlene. Half off until everything settles down."

She blinked then frowned. "I don't need charity, Tyler."

"I know you don't," he said, then put his hand on her arm. "But the company doesn't need that money right now. And you need some time for yourself, not worrying about cash and court fees and whatever."

She swallowed. Her blue eyes had moistened. "Thanks, Ty. I owe you."

# Chapter Three

"The Dunnington Arms was where we went on the piss when we were kids," Tyler said as they climbed back into the car. "We thought it was great, 'cause they served us without ID. It was only when we got older we realized it wasn't just underage drinking going on in there."

Damon was looking at the pub's web listing on his phone. "It's been raided three times for drugs in the last two years. Dozens of arrests for drunk and disorderly and assault. Shut down twice but always re-opened within a month."

"The owners pay off the right people," Tyler said, frowning. "It never stays shut long. I'm telling you, if our list of arseholes have something in common, it's the Dunnington Arms."

"People talk when they drink," Damon said. "This is where he's finding them."

"Yep," said Tyler, starting the engine.

"It opens at four," Damon said. "I'll meet you there?"

Tyler shook his head as he pulled out into the traffic. "No. We go after dark. Catch him in the act."

"That's not a good idea."

"How else are we supposed to catch him?"

"We need to be smart about this," Damon said quietly. "Ask questions...discreetly. Find out more about his habits, his weaknesses. Trust me. This is what I do."

"You do what you want. I'm going after dark."

Damon sighed. "Well, I'm not letting you do that alone, if that's what you're thinking. Just please at least wait for me before you start poking around, okay?"

Tyler looked over at the man. He was gazing earnestly at him, all traces of wryness gone from his face.

"Okay," Tyler said. "I'll wait."

* * * *

Tyler did as he'd been told, waiting outside the grimy single-story pub for Damon to show as soon as it got dark. But his patience was wearing thin by the time Damon pulled into the carpark in an unmarked white van. However, he'd styled his hair with some kind of fragrant product and had put on a skin-tight shirt and jeans, and Tyler's impatience withered like cut grass in the sun. Damon flashed his smile as he approached, then they made for the entrance.

Tyler was assaulted by a confusing mix of emotions as he stepped in the door of the Dunnington Arms. They'd put down new carpets at some point in the last ten years, but that was the only change he could see. It was still packed with people like it had been when he had been a teenager, many already too worse for wear, laughing, shouting and swearing loudly enough to make the clamor in the low-ceilinged room almost unbearable. Even the smell was the same—spilled beer and stale bodies.

Several pairs of eyes landed and stayed on them as he and Damon elbowed their way to the bar.

"A pint, mate," Tyler said to the barman then looked at Damon.

"Water, please," Damon said, scanning the bar with those hypnotic, silver-gray eyes.

"It's a pub, Damon," Tyler muttered.

"We're not on a date," Damon replied without pausing in his examination of the room. "I need to stay sharp."

"And a water," Tyler said. The barman served without comment, and they wove over to a table from which they could see the whole room.

"He's a dealer," Tyler muttered, nodding at a grim-faced character watching two teenagers playing pool with a dark intensity. "This one's a scam artist," he went on, indicating a woman sipping a large gin and showing an older man something on an iPad. "And I can see at least three enforcers for one of the local gangs. This place is a cesspit."

"An opinion I think shared by our mutual friend," Damon said in a low voice, tapping notes into his phone. "Stay focused. We're here to watch. Nothing more."

"Feels like we're the ones being watched."

Damon looked at him sharply. "What do you mean?"

Tyler unstuck his mouth with some beer, lifting his gaze from the crowd to the dark windows. "You don't feel it?"

Damon followed his gaze. "What's out back?"

"Smoking area..." Tyler froze. He'd been staring at it the whole time. Someone was standing at the window, staring in. Staring at *him*. Someone with red eyes.

Tyler stood so fast he knocked his stool over.

"Tyler? What is it? Tyler, no, wait—"

But Tyler was already pushing through the crowd. He shoved open the fire exit and rushed out into the concrete yard. It was empty but for some rotting picnic benches and a bucket overflowing with fag butts. It smelt of sun-warmed concrete and old smoke. And...something else.

*Copper. Warm wine.*

He turned, his pulse thundering, but there was no one in sight.

"Tyler, what did you see?" Damon said urgently as he joined him.

"You must have seen him, too," Tyler said, pacing the boundary of the yard, peering around the corner of the building into the carpark. "He was right here."

"Lucien?" Damon's face had changed. All the charm was gone. Blank watchfulness replaced it. "You saw him?"

"That's what I said, wasn't it?" Tyler turned again, still searching the empty lot then he paused. He wandered over to the wire fence and stared through it to the dark building beyond. "Of course."

"What is it?" Damon said, pulling out a torch and casting a light over the building. The door and windows were boarded up, the plywood scrawled with graffiti.

"This place has been shut up since I was a kid," Tyler said. "An old townhouse. No one's ever torn it down or done it up."

"It's in remarkably good condition for an abandoned building," Damon said thoughtfully, shining the torch over the brickwork and sloping roof. "Gutters clear. The roof has fresh slates."

"This is where he's hiding," Tyler said, stepping back and scanning the fence. "I know it."

"The property listing says it's owned by some corporation," Damon said, peering at his phone. "But I never heard of a corporation hanging onto prime-location property they didn't need in this climate." He examined the building again. "It could very well be an unregistered hide."

"A what?"

"Somewhere haemos bed down in the day," Damon explained. "Dark. Secure. Pretty much human-proof." He scowled. "They're supposed to be registered, assessed, legal." He shook his head. "People don't realize how much these vamps do behind our backs. How close by they can be without us even knowing."

Tyler grabbed the wire fence and started to climb.

"Tyler, wait. This isn't—"

"I'm going in," he said, swinging himself over the top and dropping to the pitted tarmac beyond. "You can come or you can stay. Whatever."

Tyler was already headed for the boarded entrance before he heard Damon's reply. He searched for a way to get at the door, but the barrier was secured tight.

Damon muttered as he climbed over the fence. "There probably isn't a way in on the ground floor," he said as he stepped up and cast his torch beam over the blocked door.

"There must be," Tyler said, pacing around the building, trying the boards on all the windows. "How else does he get in and out?"

"Probably from an upstairs window," Damon said. "Maybe even the roof."

"That's crazy."

"They're not like us. Don't really need stairs."

"They don't fly," Tyler stated, rattling the bars on a side door. He paused. "Do they?"

Damon winced. "Not as far as we know. But they can climb and find ways in and out of places we never could."

Tyler felt like he was again frozen in his living room, staring at Lucien's outline against his window.

"Listen to me," Damon said carefully. "We come back in the day. He's vulnerable when it's light. If this is really where he's hiding out..." His teeth glinted in the torchlight. "We got him."

Tyler opened his mouth but then the sound of a shoe scraping over gravel made him spin around.

Someone was standing behind them. They were so motionless it could almost be mistaken for a shadow...almost. They weren't tall, but Tyler could sense the power of the presence like static in the air. In the darkest part of the shadows two red eyes were glowing. Hot coals. Blood under a cold sunset.

Tyler's stomach dipped. He thought he'd been ready. He'd done nothing but think about this moment for months. But now it was here, and he couldn't move. Fear as potent as electricity crackled through his every cell, rendering his muscles useless. His brain seized. The thing continued to stare at him out of the blackness, unmoving.

"Tyler, go."

Tyler blinked until sense returned. Damon was holding a gun. There were several pained heartbeats where all he could do was stand there, trying to fight air into his lungs.

"Tyler, I told you...*run.*"

The command in Damon's tone freed Tyler's legs. His knees buckled, but then he got control. He ran. He didn't stop, didn't think. He pelted for the wire fence and scrambled over. He heard running footsteps behind him. Adrenaline gave him a burst of speed. Then Damon grabbed his shoulder.

"This way," Damon said, steering him toward the van. They tumbled in, and Damon slammed it into gear then accelerated out of the car park.

Tyler panted as he checked all the mirrors over and over, but there was no one behind them.

"Shit," Tyler swore and hit the dash. "Shit, shit. I choked. He was *right there,* and I bloody choked."

"You didn't choke, Tyler," Damon said in a grim tone. "You reacted to a predator."

"It was spineless. Why didn't you take him out? You had a gun."

"Unless you get a direct hit, shooting them just makes them mad," Damon barked. "And you've not seen mad until you've seen haemo-bloodlust-mad."

"We were so close—"

"We were *too* close. I'm amazed we're both still breathing, Tyler. From now on we do it my way. Understand?"

Tyler stared out of the windshield, goosebumps rippling over his skin. "He... He just stood there. Why?"

"He let us go," Damon responded after a long, careful moment.

"*Let* us?" Tyler said, straightening in his seat. "Why?"

"I don't know," Damon's voice was hard as ice. "But I doubt we'll get so lucky next time."

Tyler rubbed his face. The adrenaline was draining out of him, leaving him shaky and sick. And something else. *Disappointment?* He shook his head. "Where are we going, anyway?"

"Somewhere safe."

They drove in silence for over an hour, out of the city, into the winding country lanes. The dark was like a solid thing pressing in around them. Finally, Damon turned in through an automated gate and up to a stark cinder-block building surrounded by eye-achingly bright security lights.

The glare made Tyler's head ache as they made for a forbidding metal door.

"What the hell is this place?"

Damon didn't answer, instead pushed a buzzer.

"Hey, Larny. It's Damon."

There was a whirr as a camera over the door focused first on Damon then Tyler.

"Who's your friend?" asked a crackled voice from the intercom.

"A client," Damon said, "on the wrong side of the local bloodsucker."

There was a breathless pause during which Tyler tried to decipher the look on Damon's face then the door buzzed, and Damon pushed it open. Tyler hurried after him into a cool, dim interior. A fat man with a box of pastries sat in a booth just inside the door, surrounded by computer monitors. He gave Damon a nod as they passed. They moved along a utilitarian corridor, past a room occupied by a number of people with somber expressions bent over tables. Tyler stopped in the doorway. They were stripping and cleaning weapons—knives, guns and a few things Tyler didn't even recognize.

"Tyler." Damon stood at the end of the corridor with a hand on a banister. Tyler moved on hurriedly.

"Where the fuck are we, Damon?'"

"We call it The Fort," Damon said as he led them up two flights of stairs and onto a long corridor with many shut doors. "Somewhere we can stay safe, secure."

"From what?"

Damon tapped a code into another keypad and one of the doors opened. They moved through into a small, stark room. There was a wardrobe, a bed, a chair, a sink. No windows. No pictures on the walls, no books, no clothes.

"Specifically?" Damon said, sitting on the chair and pulling off his shoes. "Haemophiles. Though that's not on the property deeds, of course." He put his elbows on his knees and looked at Tyler. "I'm trusting you, bringing you here. It's not somewhere that usually admits strangers."

"I don't understand," Tyler said, staring round. "Is this where you live?"

"Sometimes," Damon said, leaning back in the chair and crossing his long legs at the ankle. "It's basic. But it's surrounded by daylight flood lights. Even the roof. No haemophile can get anywhere near it."

"And the characters downstairs?"

"People like me...and you. People who don't feel safe in the world right now."

Tyler shifted uncomfortably.

"We will be safe from Lucien here," Damon went on smoothly. "Then tomorrow, we'll go back to that house, when the sun's at its highest."

"He knows we've found his hiding place," Tyler said, scuffing his foot on the floor. "He'll be long gone by now."

"Most likely," Damon said, standing. "But he may have left some trace, something to indicate where he's gone—or where he's come from." He took a step forward and startled Tyler by putting his hands on his arms. "I understand, Tyler," he said softly. His face was once again warm and inviting. "It's okay to be scared. These things...? They aren't natural. And they're dangerous. But you're not alone anymore."

Tyler's heart thundered in his chest. He could smell Damon's cinnamon hair product and citrusy skin. His mouth filled with saliva at the sight of his lips so close to his own. He watched Damon read his face, and his eyes heated.

"We're staying here overnight...together?" Tyler rasped.

"It's safest that way," Damon whispered.

"There's only one bed."

"Is that a problem?"

Tyler swallowed.

Damon ran a finger down Tyler's face then under his chin. "You're an extremely attractive man, Tyler," he murmured. "And I take care of my clients. Anything you need to help you feel safe, protected...relaxed. I'm willing to be part of that."

"I don't know what I need any more," Tyler said, his voice tight and raw.

"How about we figure it out together?" Damon leaned in to kiss him.

Tyler pushed him back. They stared at each other. His throat had closed over in panic, but his skin was on fire. There was a visible bulge in the front of Damon's jeans, and Tyler's own pants were becoming too tight to bear. But his palms itched. His skin was over-sensitive, like one large healing burn.

"What do you want, Tyler?" Damon whispered.

Tyler swallowed. He sat shakily on the bed. When he spoke, his voice was harsh. "I want to watch."

Damon's eyes glinted. His lips curved. "Watch what?"

"Watch you...touch yourself."

Damon's smile widened. "You're the boss."

Damon slowly pulled his T-shirt over his head. Tyler gasped as Damon's toned, slim chest and abdomen were revealed. His skin was the color of strong coffee. There were a few silver scars crisscrossing his ribs that pulled and shrank as his muscles moved. His nipples were a warm brown, sharp with the cool air. His lips parted as he took in the look on Tyler's face, ran a hand over his chest and fingered a nipple.

"Like this?" he whispered.

Tyler nodded dumbly, wrestling his fly open and pulled out his pulsing cock. "More," he managed, pumping his erection as Damon ran his other hand down his belly.

"More, huh?" Damon's face filled with color. His eyes were locked with Tyler's. He rubbed both his nipples at once. His eyes fluttered shut, and a moan escaped his mouth. Tyler's cock jumped in his hand.

"Fuck," Tyler gasped. "Get your cock out."

Damon leaned his head back against the wall, exposing a long column of gorgeous neck. "But I'm only just getting started," he whispered, then grasped the bulge in his pants. He gasped and arched off the wall.

Tyler beat himself faster. Sweat began to prickle under his clothing. Lightning began to gather under his balls. His skin was so raw it was almost sore. He imagined the taste of Damon's skin, or the feel of those long-fingered hands on his cock. But watching him like this heated Tyler's blood more than anything real could.

"More, Damon."

Damon opened his eyes. He was still fingering one nipple and kneading his crotch through his jeans. "Tell me, Tyler," he said huskily, dropping his eyes to watch Tyler's hand as he stroked himself. "Is it the watching?" He slowly undid the button of his jeans. "Or the *being* watched that you like?"

Tyler couldn't answer. His eyes were riveted on Damon's hands. He unzipped his jeans and slid them both into his underwear. He groaned and closed his eyes again, pushing into his hands. Tyler watched him stroke himself inside his clothing with thunder roaring in his head.

"Jesus…" Tyler pumped himself harder. His mouth was dry. "Damon, I want to see it."

Damon gave him a wicked smile then shoved his jeans and underwear to his knees. Tyler inhaled sharply at the sight of his thick, swollen member, flushed with blood, framed by dark hair and damp at the tip, begging to be touched.

Damon didn't have to be told this time. Tyler watched he began to masturbate with long, slow strokes. He began to make more noises and to lean more against the wall as his legs started to shake.

"Tyler," he breathed. "Tyler, I'm imagining this is you," He closed his eyes and tilted his head back. "These are your hands. This is you touching me… This is you bringing me so close, so close…*ah*."

Damon started to come. Long, white strings of cum shot into the air, over his hands and onto the floor. Tyler could smell the sudden saltiness in the air, and that, combined with the open-mouthed mask of ecstasy contorting Damon's face, was all it took to send Tyler crashing into his own orgasm. He leaned forward, groaning, his own cum splattering his jeans and the floor. His whole body seemed to cramp around the release, tight and hot. He blinked his eyes open. Damon had pulled up his trousers and was cleaning up the mess with a towel. He held it out to Tyler, who sheepishly wiped what he could off himself and his clothing. Damon washed his hands in the sink with a smile.

"A pleasant interlude. Now we sleep," he said and clicked off the light. The room was plunged into utter darkness. Tyler listened to him strip then the bed dipped as he climbed in. Damon laid a hand on his shoulder. Tyler jerked and pulled out of reach. Damon sighed.

"Okay. I won't touch you, Tyler. Not if you don't want me to. Just try to get some rest."

Tyler took off his shoes then lay on top of the covers, fully clothed, turned away from Damon. The warmth and smell of him so close was both comforting and unnerving. Tyler still didn't know how to feel. The uncertainty was like a blade in his gut. He couldn't get comfortable.

"I used to know what I wanted," he said softly into the dark. It was easier to talk when he couldn't see Damon's face. "Took it…with whoever was willing to give it. I never thought much about it…about anything. But since that vamp attacked me… It's like I can't stop thinking…ever."

"You still know what you want, Tyler," Damon said softly after such a long silence Tyler was convinced he'd already fallen asleep. "We all face things in our lives that change what we need from people. If you stop fighting whatever this is in you that's changed, it will all be easier."

Tyler didn't answer. Soon he heard the rhythmic sound of Damon's breathing lulling into that of sleep. He felt his own muscles relax, one by one, but sleep still eluded him. He stared into the darkness as the hours slipped by.

\* \* \* \*

Damon made coffee and toast for them in the sparse kitchen on the ground floor the next morning. Tyler thought he looked far too good in bare feet, a vest and jeans to be in this place with its concrete floors, windowless walls and morose, watchful occupants. But when they were back in their room, and Damon was tucking his gun into his waistband and pulling his T-shirt over to hide it, Tyler finally began to wonder what exactly he'd got himself into.

The sun was high and hot when they left The Fort. Tyler was already sweating as they approached Damon's van.

Traffic slowed as they reached the city. Damon took a roundabout route through backstreets to the Dunnington Arms. Before reaching the pub, he turned down an alley barely wide enough to accommodate the van and stopped at the side door of the boarded-up townhouse. It looked so innocuous in the daylight, just a brick three-story building with MDF over the windows and graffiti all over the walls. It could be any empty building on any backstreet in any city in the country. But Tyler glanced at the spot where Lucien had stood, silent and watching, and his skin tingled.

They made a circuit of the building on foot but still couldn't find any way in or out. Damon didn't speak as they returned to the van. Tyler heard him rooting around in the back, then he produced a crowbar.

"What if it's alarmed?" Tyler said, looking around nervously as Damon made for the door.

"Haemophiles don't need alarm systems," Damon said, wedging the crowbar behind the board.

The board came away from the wall with a loud crack. Tyler winced and glanced around again, but they were still alone. He helped Damon move the board away, then he was kneeling to peer into the keyhole.

"Looks old," Tyler observed, taking in the peeling varnish and a tarnished metal knocker.

"Love old locks," Damon said as he pulled out some tools from his pocket. "Lovely and tactile. Don't make them like this anymore. Shame."

Damon inserted the pick tools into the lock. There were a few moments of intense concentration, then a click and the door swung open. Damon produced a torch and pulled the door wider.

"Stay behind me," he instructed, and they drifted in.

The interior was dusty, dark and surprisingly cool. Tyler blinked as his eyes adjusted to the gloom, but all he could make out were bare floors, a rotting staircase and an empty brick fireplace. Damon was examining the floorboards with his torch. The dust was even and undisturbed.

"Shall we try upstairs?"

"They go underground if they can. There." Damon's torch beam had lit on a door half-hidden behind a threadbare curtain. It, too, was locked, but Damon picked it and opened the door onto a brick staircase leading down into the dark. It got colder as they descended. Their steps echoed in the stillness.

"Definitely an unregistered hide," Damon said. He spoke softly, but it still sounded too loud in the close, secret space. "Once we're done here, we'll report it and get it destroyed. They're not supposed to—" He stopped speaking as he stepped off the bottom step. Tyler leaned to peer over his shoulder.

A large metal box, like a chest freezer but bigger, stood in the middle of the otherwise empty basement. It was so still and silent in the room, the box looked sinister, though Tyler couldn't explain why.

"That's where he—?"

"Shh." Damon made an urgent motion with his hand.

Tyler's flesh crawled. "You think he's *in* there?" he whispered, pulse quickening.

"I'd be happier if the lid was open," Damon said so softly Tyler barely heard him. "Then we'd know he'd moved on."

"There's no way he stayed here," Tyler murmured. "Not after last night."

"Maybe he has nowhere else to go. And this is a high-grade sleep cell. New, too. I doubt he'd just leave it here."

"Well, let's fucking check then." Tyler put his hand out and Damon grabbed his wrist.

"Are you insane?"

"What? It's day," Tyler said. "Like you said, he's helpless. Right?"

"I never said he'd be *helpless*," Damon said, not releasing Tyler's wrist. "I said he'd be *vulnerable*. We have the advantage right now, sure. But only if we *don't* wake him up."

"Why?"

"He'd rip our throats out before we'd even drawn breath to yell. So, please…*don't* open the lid."

Tyler swore and took a shaky step back from the cell. "So, what do we *do*?"

Damon smiled. "I'll show you."

Damon set Tyler to work helping him haul ropes, trolleys, flood lights and other equipment from his van to the basement. Soon the room was lit as brightly as the summer day outside. Dust motes danced in the air. The metal box gleamed white.

"The lights buy us some time if the worst should happen," Damon said. "But we need to move fast."

"Wait," Tyler said as Damon set up a hydraulic trolley. "We're taking the whole thing out of here?"

"Exactly," Damon said, gesturing to the box. "Help me tilt it so I can get this underneath."

"What about all that stuff about him ripping our throats out if we wake him?"

"We'll be safe as long as the lid stays shut, like I said," Damon said. "Now, come one. This'll be our only chance, Tyler."

Tyler hesitated then joined Damon around the other side of the sleeping cell. They tilted it off the floor and got the trolley under it. Tyler was sweating, despite the coolness of the room. Damon activated the lifters, and it groaned and hissed. Slowly, the cell was lifted from the floor. He maneuvered it toward the stairs.

Damon tapped at the trolley's controls and, slowly and laboriously, it commenced clunking the huge metal sleep cell up the stairs, one step at a time. It seemed to take an eternity, and with every clunking movement, Tyler was ready for something to come tearing out of the box and slash his throat to the bone. But, somehow, they reached the ground floor and steered the trolley across the rattling floorboards and out into the sunshine.

Damon opened the back of the van and lowered a loading plate. Tyler stared inside. There were racks and racks of equipment, tools, more floodlights, electric cable…and weapons.

"What is all this?"

"You ain't seen nothing yet," Damon said with another lop-sided grin as the cell stopped level with the back of the van. Damon steered the trolley in, hopped back out and locked the van doors.

"Come on," he said.

"Where are we taking him?"

"Just get in, Tyler," Damon commanded. "We'll run out of daylight."

Tyler obeyed, dazed. Damon steered into the city traffic with the ease of someone doing the school run. Tyler sat stiff in his seat. The presence behind the thin metal wall dividing the driving compartment from the back of the van pulsed in his brain and flesh. He couldn't even bring himself to ask any questions until they were out of the city and heading north.

"Where are we going now?"

"You'll see," Damon said and continued to drive. The hard, intent look was back in his eyes. It made his face look less fey and more demonic. Tyler suppressed a shiver.

The roads Damon took got narrower and narrower until they were following something that was little more than a track.

It ended in a sudden, sharp turn and a large, iron gate. Damon tapped something on his phone and the gate groaned and began to rumble open. They drove into the shade of some close-growing trees. Tyler could make out a shape between the trunks ahead. A building — small, single-story, with walls of corrugated iron. There was a single door and just enough space between it and the trees to park the van.

"What the hell is this?" Tyler said, eyeing the place with an unpleasant sensation in his gut. "Another Fort?"

"Oh no," Damon said with a grin. "Much more interesting. Come on. We need to get our prize inside before it starts to get dark."

Tyler's stomach clenched as he helped Damon get the sleeping cell out of the van and steer it toward the building.

"What are we doing, Damon? Do we even know he's in there?"

"Oh, he's in there," Damon said in a loaded tone as he swiped a card in the locking mechanism on the heavy-duty door. "I weighed it."

"Fuck," Tyler said, staring at the smooth, metal lid with ice and fire snaking through his insides.

"Don't worry," Damon said as he pushed the door open. "This is literally the safest place you can be right now. Come on. Help me get him inside."

# Chapter Four

Tyler steered the trolley through the door as Damon guided it from the front. Inside was a whitewashed room, brightly lit and empty, apart from a large lift in the corner.

"Is that...?"

"Our workshops have to be underground," Damon said as he wheeled the trolley toward the lift. "You'll see why soon enough."

Tyler stood in the lift with Damon and Lucien's sleeping cell, dizzy with confusion and uncertainty. The temperature dropped so suddenly that Tyler shivered. The doors opened on a bright hall. The air tasted thin and clinical. Damon steered the trolley across the hall and through a thick, steel door. They were in a bright, white room — more of a cell. The floor was concrete. There was a large mirror on one side. Tyler had seen the inside of enough police interview rooms to recognize it as one-way glass. A TV screen was embedded in the wall to his right, otherwise it was featureless. Damon unloaded the sleeping cell then steered the trolley and Tyler back out. The metal door clunked shut behind them, and there was a series of clicks as several locks slammed home. Damon left the trolley against the wall and beckoned Tyler to follow him.

They went through another door into a room filled with computer monitors and controls. On one wall was a wide window overlooking the room they'd just left. The sleeping cell stood, undisturbed, in the middle of the clean, white space. But that wasn't that Tyler was looking at.

He stared, frozen, at the wall on his left. A series of hooks and shelves held a dizzying array of weaponry — flails, knives, guns, goggles, helmets, body armor. It put the collection in Damon's van to shame.

"Tools of the trade," Damon said, following Tyler's gaze.

"Who the fuck *are* you, man?" he breathed.

"Someone who is good at their job."

Tyler shook his head. "This is insane."

"Why do you think my fees are so high?" Damon replied, taking a seat at the computer desk and tapping the keyboards. "Environmental controls are all online. Safety protocols engaged." He grinned at Tyler. "We did it, Tyler. We got him."

Tyler blinked at the closed sleep cell with a lump in his throat. "What now?"

"Now we wait." Damon toggled a control on the panel in front of him and the light in the room beyond the window dimmed then brightened. "More daylight floods," Damon explained. "Once he's awake and out of the box, we can control him with these. He'll still be dangerous" — Damon gave him a warning look — "but we're in control now. You can take all the time you want to decide how you want to do it."

"Do what?" Tyler said carefully.

Damon nodded to the wall of weaponry. "Whatever you want. Quick or slow. Painless or...not." Damon grinned again. Tyler suddenly realized how sharp his canines were. "Whatever you need."

Tyler stared at the sleeping cell, his body rigid. "You mean...kill him?"

Damon blinked, face slack with surprise. "Isn't that what you wanted?"

"I...I dunno."

Damon regarded him in silence for a long time. "What did you think we'd do with him after we caught him, Tyler?"

Tyler shifted. "I don't *know*. Hand him over to the cops?"

"The police can't do anything with one like this," Damon insisted. "He's old, strong, basically primeval. The only way to deal with haemos like this is..." Damon dragged a thumb across his throat.

Tyler stared at him. "You've done this before, haven't you?"

"Tyler. This is what I *do*." He gestured around him. "That's what this place is *for*. You can't destroy them while they're sleeping. It's too dangerous. This whole setup"—he indicated the cell—"is so that when they wake up, they are contained and can be dealt with using less risk."

Tyler couldn't tear his gaze away from Damon's hard eyes. "And what's the TV for?"

Damon gestured to a camera on the control board. "I usually interrogate them first. Find out what I can. Where their illegal communes are. Their unregistered hides. Who they've killed. I have been able to supplement several official Kill Lists."

"Kill Lists?"

"The government holds a list of every registered haemophile's known victims. It's supposed to help them monitor and manage them." His face darkened. "Though they don't do enough, which is why people like me have to do what they don't have the guts to handle."

"How many?" Tyler said, voice quiet. "How many of them have you done?"

"Don't look so shocked," Damon replied softly. "I protect innocent people...like you. It's what you hired me for."

"How *many*?"

"Have I killed, specifically?" Damon looked away. "None, as it happens. They've always managed to escape. But not this time."

Tyler stared into the white room with his flesh crawling.

"I've been preparing for this for a long time, Tyler," Damon said, stretching out in the chair, his sinewy body rippling through his thin clothing. "I assure you I'm quite capable. But you're the client." He gestured at the cell again. "I'll leave this one to you, if that's what you want."

Tyler shifted from one foot to the other. The atmosphere suddenly felt stifling.

Damon sighed and rested his elbows on his knees, leaning forward to look him in the eye. "You can build up to it if you want. He's not going anywhere, trust me. And a specimen as old as this one...? There's a lot he could tell us."

Tyler unstuck his tongue with an effort. "What makes you think he'll talk to us?"

"I'm good at making them talk." His grin widened. "Don't you see, Tyler? We're in control here. *You* now have power over *him*. You can do whatever you want — whatever you need to feel safe again."

Damon stood. He was careful not to touch Tyler, but he brought his mouth close to his face, his breath warm on Tyler's lips. "I can help you figure out what you want."

He took Tyler's hand. Tyler started but didn't pull away. His blood was on fire. Damon pressed Tyler's hand to the front of his jeans. Tyler felt the hard flesh there and shivered.

"I'm here for you," Damon whispered. "Whatever you need."

He leaned in and brushed his lips over Tyler's face. Tyler flinched, but he didn't pull away. "We're the same, Tyler. I'll show you that."

Damon smelled of cinnamon and clean sweat. Tyler could feel the heat of his skin, even though clothing and air separated them. Tension was strung through his body like hot wire, but his cock still jumped in his pants. It had all been too long…too emotional. And his body had been aching for…*something* for months — something he hadn't been able to give it.

Damon locked his eyes on Tyler's and began to rub Tyler's hand against his clothed erection. "Want to watch me jerk off again?" he whispered.

Tyler shook his head and stepped back, even though his own pants were uncomfortably tight. "That thing is right there," he forced out and gestured through the window. "It's not safe."

"We're safe," Damon stated. "Wait until he wakes up. Then I can prove it to you."

Tyler swallowed. His throat was dry. He couldn't find an answer.

Damon went to the door and opened it. "Come on. Don't know about you, but I'm famished."

Tyler had never had less appetite in his life, but he was relieved to leave the room.

He followed Damon down the hall and through a series of security doors. "I take no chances," he said as he opened the last one and ushered Tyler into a large living space. The walls were blank white, but there was a large bed against one wall and a well-equipped kitchen unit against the other. Another corner contained a sofa, television and a desk with a high-end computer. Everything was spotlessly clean, and when Damon opened the fridge, Tyler was surprised to see it was full of fruit, vegetables and fresh meat.

"So *this* is where you live? Not The Fort?"

"The Fort is a bolt-hole," Damon said, setting lettuce, cold chicken and olive oil on the counter. "When you need to get away, fast. This is where I live, mostly, when I'm not on the road."

"I'm not really hungry," Tyler said as Damon got two plates out of the cupboard.

Damon tilted his head, giving Tyler a look, half impatience, half pity. Then he moved to the desk, unlocked it with a key from around his neck and drew out a file. He selected a piece of paper and held it out. "Perhaps this will help settle your stomach."

Damon took the paper.

*Confidential–*
*International Assembly for Haemophile Affairs –*
*Confirmed Kill List of Subject Known as 'Lucien'*
*Subject Status: Unregistered*

*Classification:    A — Unpredictable,    Uncooperative, Extremely Dangerous*

The long list of names below this header blurred in front of Tyler's eyes. The dates that went with them spanned over hundreds of years, dozens of countries.

"The unofficial list is much longer," Damon said.

Tyler cleared his throat. "Unofficial?"

"Suspected kills they can't prove. But I've studied them...and him. I know he did them."

"Some of these are recent," Tyler said, his voice raw. "Last year, even."

"Uh-huh," Damon took the list back, slid it into the file and laid it on the desk. "He never stopped. Never joined a commune. Never registered himself or even gave anyone his real name, as far as I can tell. The only reason we know he exists at all is through the reports of other haemophiles — and from you." Damon turned to face him with his arms folded. "Your name could have been on that list, too, Tyler. You need to remember that."

"But it isn't," Tyler said, frowning, disquiet snaking under his skin. "He killed all these people. Why not me?"

Damon raised an eyebrow. "Maybe we can ask him. But first" — he turned back to the kitchen — "we eat. We need to keep our strength up. This isn't going to be an easy task."

"What isn't?"

Damon started chopping tomatoes. "Lucien is the oldest one I've ever known — ever heard of, even." Damon went to the fridge for parmesan and a lemon. "And they get stronger as they get older...and stranger, harder for humans to communicate with." He chopped the lemon in half with a large knife and squeezed the juice onto the food. "It's frustrating. He'll know so much that could be useful. But we may not get anything from him, in which case we are better off getting rid of him sooner rather than later."

Tyler sat on the sofa and stared at the wall in silence as Damon continued to prepare the meal. He ate it mechanically, even though some distant part of his brain acknowledged the Caesar salad was exceptionally good. Damon kept his distance and didn't speak again.

He left the room after they'd eaten, instructing Tyler not to leave. Tyler turned on the TV, but he couldn't concentrate. Instead, he watched the clock count the minutes toward nightfall with a twisted expectancy in his stomach that he couldn't untangle.

When he could no longer sit still, he drifted to the desk and opened the file again. As well as Lucien's Kill List, it contained newspaper articles, police reports and more official documents from the International Assembly for Haemophile Affairs that Tyler couldn't decipher.

He turned again to the Kill List, trying to process it, telling himself to really see the long, long list of murders Lucien had committed, going back centuries. He groped after the fury that had haunted him ever since the dreadful moment out on Askham Moor. This should have fed it, should have brought it back to life.

But all he could think of was Lucien's voice in his ear, his breath on his neck. He shivered and made himself focus on the names, on the strange feeling that tickled through him as he read. He frowned, reading them again, chasing the feeling.

"Tyler?" Tyler jumped. Damon was in the doorway. He was frowning at him thoughtfully. "Five minutes to sunset."

Tyler set the file aside and followed Damon to the observation room. Damon sat at the desk, his face hard, his eyes calculating. The white room beyond the glass was the same as when they'd left it. The sleeping cell was still shut.

Tyler lowered himself into another chair. One of Damon's machines buzzed at twenty-three minutes after twenty hours.

"That's sunset." Damon's face was set. His gaze was fixed through the glass.

Tyler's palms itched. He held his breath.

Nothing happened.

Several breathless minutes passed. Damon still didn't move. He checked the readings on his computer monitors but nothing changed.

Tyler shifted in his seat. A strange disappointment ghosted through him.

"Perhaps it's empty after all…"

Damon didn't reply. He sat motionless, blank-faced, unmoving. Tyler took a breath to repeat himself when he heard a soft click.

Tyler froze. The lid of the cell had lifted perhaps an inch. Again, for several more minutes, nothing happened. Tyler's shoulders were tightening to the point of pain when slim, pale fingers appeared in the gap. They had fingernails as long and as sharp as talons, glass-clear, curved and deadly-looking. They curled around the lid and lifted it high…then stopped. The fingers disappeared. Tyler's heart thumped in his chest.

"What's happening?"

Damon didn't answer. He was staring. Tyler wasn't sure if he was even aware he was there.

Finally, the lid was pushed vertically. Out slid a lithe figure—one leg, then an arm, then a body. His feet touched the concrete floor. He straightened, his back to the window, movements liquid as a dancer's. His straight, black hair fell in a smooth curtain down his back. It reflected the overhead lights as if it had been glossed. He wore a floor-length black coat, marred here and there with dust. His hands hung at his sides, the skin bone-white against the black wool.

His head moved as he took in the door, the TV screen, the blank walls.

Finally, he turned.

Tyler had thought seeing Lucien clearly would make him less terrifying. Now he longed to slam at the controls on Damon's desk until he found the switch to plunge the room into darkness. The illumination washed Lucien's skin so pale it was almost translucent, so white it was almost blue. There were no age lines in his face, no stubble on his jaw, no folds in his skin. His eyebrows were perfect, black arches. His cheekbones were sharp, his jaw so defined it could have been sculpted. The lines of his unsmiling mouth had the look of purposeful, if melancholy, design. He looked carved from marble and was almost as lifeless.

Apart from his eyes...ruby-red, glowing, like fire, they were fringed by thick, black lashes and were so deep it was like standing on the edge of an ocean of blood. They appeared to fix on Tyler, even through the one-way glass, and stayed there, unblinking.

He wore a black jumper under the coat, black trousers and shoes. The only thing that wasn't black was the crisp collar of a white shirt, whiter than snowfall and yet not even coming close to the complex paleness of his smooth, unblemished skin.

Tyler fought to get breath into his body. The haemophile was all at once utterly frightful and paralyzingly beautiful. Tyler couldn't grasp the tumbling sensations that avalanched through him.

It was several moments before even Damon moved. He reached out a shaking hand and flicked a desk on the control desk.

"Lucien, I believe?"

The crimson eyes slid from Tyler to Damon. Damon flicked the switch off again. "He can't see anything," he said in a low voice. "He's just trying to scare us."

*It's working.* Tyler stopped the words leaving his mouth by clenching his jaw.

Damon flicked the switch back. "I have someone here who has something to say to you," he said. Lucien's eyes stayed on Damon. Damon nodded to Tyler. "Go on," he murmured.

Tyler took a shaking breath.

"Lucien," he managed, the word tasting strange and strong in his mouth. "I'm guessing you remember me?"

It was several long, silent moments before Lucien's impossible eyes slid back toward Tyler. He still didn't speak.

"No point in playing dumb," Tyler said, finally feeling a ghost of his old anger flare. "You know who I am."

"Of course I do." His voice rippled through the speakers like a cold wind — deep and smooth as black velvet. So utterly devoid of expression and accent that there was no mistaking it came from something that was not human.

"Then you know..." Tyler's voice cracked. He swallowed, tried again. "You know why you're here."

Lucien didn't move. Didn't speak. Didn't blink. Tyler's pulse slugged in his throat and temples. He gave Damon a pleading look.

"You've murdered countless people, Lucien," Damon said and the strength in his assertion helped Tyler stop shaking. "You're here to face justice. But first—"

"Justice?" Lucien didn't speak loudly but the word still burst in the air like an explosion. "I would be interested to hear your definition of the word."

"Justice is facing consequences of your crimes," Damon went on, his voice harder. "Atoning for the fear and pain you've caused others."

"You think you understand pain, fear? You don't. Not yet."

Damon flicked the audio back off and rubbed his mouth.

"What's the matter?" Tyler asked, trying to look away from Lucien but failing. "Not scared, right?"

Damon shook his head but hesitated before he spoke. "Of course not. This facility is state-of-the-art. My latest round of improvements have made it completely haemo-proof. He can threaten us all he wants, but he's helpless here."

Damon stood a little awkwardly and clicked keys. A hidden hatch in the wall of Lucien's room opened to reveal a metal flask. Lucien didn't turn. Damon pressed the audio switch again.

"There's blood in the flask. Enjoy it while you can." He clicked it back off.

"Why are you feeding him?" Tyler asked, standing as Damon moved to a different set of controls.

"They only get more dangerous if they're hungry. And if it's going to be a while before you feel ready to face him…" Damon nodded to the weapons, and Tyler went cold. "We need to keep the situation as controlled as possible."

"I'm sure he can fucking see me," Tyler murmured, meeting Lucien's piercing gaze, which was still locked on him through the glass.

"He can't," Damon insisted. "He's just guessing to freak you out."

"Pretty good guesser," Tyler said, staring at Lucien with his scalp tightening.

Finally, Lucien moved. He turned slowly, so controlled it was almost like a slow dance without music. He paced the circumference of his prison, running his fingers over the walls. He stopped at the door and inspected it. His expression never changed, but Tyler had the unnerving sensation he was seeing right through the metal.

"He can't get out," Damon insisted. "We're safe, Tyler. Want me to prove it?"

"That would be nice, yeah."

Tyler regretted the words almost before he'd finished saying them. Damon's smile was like a twist in his face as he turned a dial on the controls. The light in the room changed, brightening but also shifting in hue.

Lucien winced and held his hands up as if to ward off a blow. Damon twisted the dial further, the cruel smile opening his lips. The light increased, and Lucien's face twisted in pain, revealing his long, sharp canines and incisors. His open mouth was very red. Tyler's heart slammed against his ribs and fear rumbled through him. But then he blinked, and Lucien was gone.

Tyler yelled and stumbled backward scrabbling for the door, but Damon grabbed his arm.

"It's fine," he insisted. "He's just back in the cell."

Tyler blinked again. The sleeping cell was shut. Damon dimmed the light. His face was hard with gratification.

"See? We're in control."

Tyler grabbed the desk to stay upright, his breathing gradually slowing.

"I doubt we'll see him again for a while now," Damon said. "Come on. Let's get a drink. You look like you need one."

Damon led the way back to the living quarters. Tyler followed, a little shakily.

"I don't understand any of this," Tyler said as he took the offered beer. He dropped onto the sofa and stared at the ceiling, deliberately not looking at the TV that Damon had tuned to a camera feed from Lucien's cell. "He saw us last night. He must have known we'd come for him. Why'd he go back to that basement?"

"It's not the first time a haemophile has underestimated humanity," Damon said, sitting next to Tyler, close enough that their legs almost touched.

Tyler examined Damon for a long moment then the image on the screen. "You really think we should kill him?"

"You wanted to make him pay." Damon turned on the sofa to face Tyler. "If it's too hard, I understand. You helped me catch him, and for that I am grateful. If you don't want to actually go any further, you can leave if you want. I can finish the job alone."

"No," Tyler said quickly, then, more controlled. "No. I need to see this through."

Tyler held Damon's bewitching gaze for a long moment. He could see his pulse in his neck and the heated look in his eyes. Tyler's blood stirred. Damon set his beer aside and shifted closer. He held out a hand and hovered it over Tyler's leg. Tyler drew a shaking breath.

"You're a strong man," Damon murmured. "Strong people find it hard not to be in control." Slowly, without breaking eye contact, Damon touched the tip of his finger to Tyler's leg then ran it up his thigh. "I understand that. I want to help you feel in control again."

The contact sparked through Tyler's tightly wound body. His groin started to throb. His mind flooded with memories of the night before. Damon's body, Damon's hooded eyes, the sound he'd made as he'd come.

"I'm thinking about it, too," Damon said softly, studying his face. He lowered his eyes to the front of Tyler's jeans, tented with his erection. "And more."

Tyler growled and pushed Damon onto the sofa. He climbed on top and thrust his hands into Damon's shirt. Damon gasped and grabbed Tyler's arse, pressing their crotches together. Tyler buried his face in Damon's shoulder, crushing his eyes shut and thrusting against him. The friction against his cock sent thunder rolling through his insides. He dug his fingers into Damon's hot flesh and shivered when Damon tightened his grip.

"Want to fuck me?" Damon breathed in his ear, lifting his hips to rub his contained erection against Tyler's belly.

Tyler lifted his head and looked into Damon's flushed face. "I…I dunno…"

Damon tried to fumble a hand into Tyler's waistband, but Tyler grabbed his wrist. They lay there, their limbs tangled, breathing heavily, staring at each other.

"You need something, Tyler," Damon breathed. "What is it?"

Tyler struggled for a response, then registered movement out the corner of his eye.

They both turned to look at the TV screen. Lucien was out of his cell. He stood stock-still, staring at the camera. The blood-red gaze lanced through Tyler, but instead of chilling the arousal from his flesh, his blood pumped hotter.

"Well, well," Damon said throatily. His smile was suggestive. "It appears we have an audience."

Tyler's mouth dried up. His cock throbbed. "Can he see us?"

Damon reached for a tablet on the coffee table. "Right now, he's probably just sensing *us* watching *him*. It's pretty fucking creepy with how much they can smell and sense, even at a distance. That's how he freaked you out through the one-way glass." Damon tapped a few controls on the tablet then held it up, his finger hovering. "But if I press this...? Yes, he will be able to see us. Would you like that?"

Tyler stared at the tablet, then at the camera in the TV frame, then at Damon's face, tight with desire, his eyes hot and wanting. Finally, he looked at Lucien, motionless as a Michelangelo sculpture, more beautiful than a Botticelli painting, more terrifying than a shadow moving in a dark, empty room.

"Let him watch," Tyler heard himself say in a voice that didn't sound like his own.

Damon grinned and tapped the tablet. Lucien's gaze lowered at the same time the light of his own screen flickered in his blood-red eyes. Tyler could almost feel the haemophile's gaze on him, burning like spilled wax.

He suddenly couldn't get Damon out of his clothes fast enough. Damon panted and tugged at Tyler's in turn, ripping seams and busting buttons. Finally, they were naked and running their hands over each other. The feel of another human being's flesh against his own had been too much, too overwhelming for too long. But now, with Lucien's eyes on him, all Tyler wanted to do was fuck…*hard*.

"Where's your stuff?" Tyler panted against Damon's neck, his eyes still fixed on the screen. Lucien hadn't moved. His expression hadn't changed. But Tyler knew, somewhere deep inside where this aching need was pulsing, that Lucien couldn't look away any more than he could.

"Here," Damon said breathily, pressing a condom and lube into Tyler's hand as he nipped at his jaw and rubbed his erection against his thigh. "Where do you want it?"

"Behind the sofa," Tyler said, "so I can see him." They scrambled upright, and Damon moved around and clutched the sofa back.

"He's still watching," Tyler said as he stepped behind Damon, his whole body trembling, pulling the condom onto his cock with shaking hands.

"Let's give him a show then," Damon said, grinning at the camera.

Tyler swallowed a desperate noise and squeezed lube onto his fingers. He leaned so close his knees kissed the back of Damon's legs, locked eyes with the camera and thrust two fingers into Damon's hot, tight entrance.

Damon groaned and arched his back, pushing onto Tyler's fingers. Tyler watched, dazed and fascinated, as Lucien swallowed. The smooth skin of his neck shifted as the muscles moved. Damon's tightness around his fingers made Tyler's flesh sing. He had to make himself prepare Damon, sweeping his fingers and stretching while Damon moaned and whimpered. Every fiber of Tyler's being wanted to plunge into Damon while Lucien watched, fuck the other man senseless while the gaze of the haemophile scoured the flesh from his bones.

"God, Tyler," Damon panted, his shoulders tensing as Tyler inserted a third finger and reached deep. He was stroking himself too, hard and fast. "Fuck. Yes. Right there."

Tyler reached again, and Damon's knees buckled. Tyler clutched his hip to keep him upright, removed his fingers and pushed his cock against the ring of muscle.

Damon let out a long, low noise of pleasure as Tyler slid into him. Tyler's whole body hovered, tight and still, on the edge of orgasm. He realized he'd closed his eyes. His chest was heaving against Damon's back.

"Move," Damon begged. "Please, Tyler."

Tyler didn't dare. He'd opened his eyes. Lucien's lips had parted, allowing Tyler a glimpse of his tantalizing mouth. His bottom lip was wet, as if he'd licked it.

A noise almost like one of pain escaped Tyler. He tilted his hips to get deeper into Damon, who moaned his name. That was all it took for Tyler to climax, the orgasm crashing through him, hard and fast, hurried and blissful and stunted, all at once. He fumbled blindly for Damon's cock, and his body clamped around him as Damon cried out and came.

They bent over the sofa, panting together, still joined, with the sweat cooling on their skin. Damon straightened, and Tyler took a stumbling step back. He felt dizzy and drained. The sated desire was heavy in his limbs, but something still felt... off. It had all happened so quickly.

Before Tyler had had time to focus again, Damon had turned the TV off. He was smiling the lazy, satisfied smile of a cat who'd just finished a saucer of cream.

"I think we've figured out what you want," he said.

"What?" Tyler asked dumbly.

Damon nodded to the TV. "You want him."

Tyler went very cold very fast. "What?"

"There's more than one way to exorcise a demon, Tyler," Damon said, coming around the sofa to lay a hand on his chest. "And with careful handling, I think we can make it happen."

Tyler pressed the heels of his palms into his eyes. "What are you saying?"

"You want to fuck Lucien. I get it," he said, spreading his hands before Tyler could protest. "Of course I do. Who wouldn't?"

"You're insane..."

"More sane than most, sadly," he said, gathering their scattered clothes. "But from the way he watched us, I'm confident we could let you play with him." He straightened and looked Tyler in the eye. "But remember, he's still a monster, no matter how fuckable he is. And our job is to stop him from hurting anyone else. Whatever else you want or need, you need to remember that. Understand?"

"I don't want to *play* with him," Tyler said firmly. "I don't want to fuck him. I want to stop him. That's all."

Damon chuckled and ran a finger over Tyler's bare chest. "You're a terrible liar, Tyler. The shower's through there," he said, gesturing to a door next to the bed and dumping their clothes on the sofa. "Then I think we better turn in. It's been a long day."

Tyler couldn't help but agree, though he suddenly hadn't the energy to summon the words to do it out loud.

He hurried into the bathroom, glad to get a closed door between himself and everything that had just happened.

# Chapter Five

Tyler woke, groggy from the depth of his sleep, to the sound and smell of Damon cooking eggs. He blinked stupidly, trying to engage his brain. He had slept like a baby, even with the unfamiliar presence of Damon at his side. He usually hated sharing a bed, only suffering it on the occasions when the sex had been good enough that he'd wanted the chance of a morning fuck before the person pissed off, out of his life forever. And while the sex with Damon had sated something, it hadn't been good enough for him, under normal circumstances, to bother sending a message, let alone spend a night.

But whatever had been building in him since that night on the moor was teetering on the edge of exploding. And fucking Damon with Lucien's eyes on him had lanced a deep, swollen need. Even knowing Lucien was just a couple of walls away made his blood stir and his morning wood twitch under the covers.

And that scared him more than anything else about this whole fucked-up situation.

"Hey there," Damon said as he set two plates on the coffee table. "Figured you'd be hungry."

Tyler found he was ravenous. He pulled on his jeans and grabbed the plate of scrambled eggs and buttered toast, sat next to Damon and started shoveling forkfuls into his mouth. Damon watched him over the rim of his coffee mug.

When his plate was empty, he found he was staring at the TV screen, his mind a confused blank.

"So…" Damon spoke quietly as he set his own plate aside, "there's not going to be anything happening around here until sunset. You want me to drop you in town?"

Tyler blinked. "You kicking me out?"

Damon raised his eyebrows. "No, though I am surprised that it would bother you."

It didn't…not in itself. But Tyler knew Lucien was sleeping somewhere in this building. And he knew he'd never find the place again if Damon didn't want him to.

"I'll come get you again later," Damon said with a sly smile. "You don't need to worry about that."

Tyler looked away. "I need a change of clothes. And I'd better check to be sure that the police haven't cottoned to all this."

"They haven't," Damon said, gathering the plates.

"How do you know?"

"I know," Damon said, putting the plates in the sink. He went to the door. "I'm going to check in on our guest's overnight readings. I'll meet you outside in ten minutes."

The urge to follow him to Lucien's cell was strong. But instead, he got dressed and, somehow, found his way back outside. The air was already hot under the trees, despite the early hour. He paced the perimeter of the building, frowning thoughtfully, but the main door appeared to be the only way in. There was no visible sign of the sprawling complex below his feet. He couldn't quite shake the uncomfortable feeling the place stirred in him.

Tyler tried to memorize the drive back to the city, but he was sure Damon took a purposefully circuitous route. He didn't have the faintest clue where they were until York started appearing on the road signs. They didn't speak as they drove, and Tyler had the distinct impression Damon was assessing his silence just as much as the other way around.

Damon dropped him outside his apartment building with an enigmatic smile and a promise to collect him before sundown.

As Tyler let himself into his flat, the uncomfortable feeling increased, making the inside of his skin itch. He drifted into his kitchen and filled his coffee machine, but his mind was still back in the woods, on the locked room and its occupant…on the wall of weaponry.

"Tyler."

Tyler swore and spun around. Emerald stood from the living room sofa. She wore a tailored dress in buttercup yellow and a stern expression.

"Jesus, Emmy," he said, thrusting a mug into the machine as it started to beep. "You scared the shit outta me."

"Where have you been?"

He frowned. "Huh?"

"You didn't come home last night."

"And how do you know that?"

Emerald lifted an eyebrow. "I know it's not unusual for you to spend your nights elsewhere, little brother. But racing out of the city in strange, unmarked vans?"

He covered his reaction with a scowl. "You got your goons following me?"

"No need," she said, folding your arms. "When you have cozy chats with enigmatic strangers in Ye Olde Starre Inn, people notice."

Tyler swore. "The landlord's one of yours."

She sighed and came into the kitchen. Her heels clicked on the tiles. "I'm not one to interfere in your life, Tyler. You know that. Can't afford to get mixed up in your mess most of the time, if nothing else." Her face grew stern. "But I'm telling you to stay away from this Damon character. He's bad news."

"How do you know Damon?" Tyler asked warily.

"Never mind how or what I know. I know enough. So I'm telling you to steer well clear of him. Understand?"

"You don't give me orders," he said, going to the fridge for milk. "I don't care what you think you know."

"I know the sort of circles he moves in," she said. "Conspiracy nuts. Haemo-haters. Climate-change deniers."

Tyler snorted, stirring milk and sugar into his coffee. "Never known you to be spooked by headcases like that."

"These are the kind with guns," she said. Tyler refused to meet her eyes. "I mean it, Tyler. These people are well connected, protected. I don't know how, but they are. And they're dangerous. This Damon character? He's one of the worst. He's well-funded and too clever by half. I'm warning you now. Whatever you think he's giving you, it's not worth it."

"You don't know what you're talking about," Tyler said after a moment's hesitation. He moved to the living room and dropped onto the sofa. "The election's got you paranoid, that's all."

"It's not paranoia to be wary when this guy blows into your city without warning," Emerald said, tilting her chin. "No one knows where he's originally from. Hell, no one even knows his real name. Whatever's brought him to our neck of the woods, I only know it can't be good."

"You weren't bothered about all those haemos blowing into town," Tyler said, watching her face.

Emerald's face hardened. "Damon has potential to do way, way more damage. And I bet you can't look me in the eye and tell me the two things aren't linked." Tyler looked away. "Thought so," Emerald said levelly. Silence fell between them. "Where is he?" Emerald said firmly. "Where's Damon hiding out? What's he told you?"

Tyler kept his mouth clenched shut. His sister's eyes hardened. "Fine." She stood. "Don't say I didn't warn you, Tyler. And don't expect me to bail you out when the shit hits the fan." She looped her handbag over her shoulder and strode for the door. She paused and turned back. "And it will hit the fan…big time. Remember I said this, little brother."

She slammed the door on her way out.

Tyler was left alone in the silent flat with the smell of Damon on his clothes, the feel of Lucien's eyes hot on his skin and his sister's words looping in his head.

\* \* \* \*

He was on the pavement outside his apartment in plenty of time for Damon to pick him up. He got into the van without hesitation and felt his skin quiver in anticipation as they drove out of the city.

Damon took another roundabout way, checking his mirrors more than was necessary. He again wore the controlled, tight expression that made his face look sinister. Tyler was grateful when they left the last streetlight behind, and the dimness obscured his features.

"He will be awake in five minutes," he said, checking his watch as they rode the lift into the underground levels of his complex. "Let's see if he's loosened up enough to answer some questions."

"What sort of questions?"

"The one question I only ever really want an answer to." Damon met his eyes. "Who he's killed." The lift doors opened, and Damon strolled out. Tyler lingered a moment before following.

"We have his Kill List," he said.

"We have his *official* list," Damon said, opening the door to the living quarters and heading for the desk to remove Lucien's file. "It barely scratches the surface." He shut the door again and took Tyler back toward the observation room. "I'll prove to the world these things can't be suffered to continue if it kills me."

Tyler's scalp prickled at the undercurrent in his voice and fell a step behind.

When they entered the observation room, the only light came from the computer screens. Beyond the glass was impenetrable black. Damon took a seat, tapped some keys and twisted a dial. Slowly, the light brightened.

The sleeping cell was open. Lucien sat against the wall. His fingers were interlaced in his lap. His legs were crossed at the ankle. His eyes were closed, the thick lashes dark against his pearl-white skin. He was as still as stone. *Stiller*. He made no reaction to their presence or the increasing light. He just sat there, motionless, silent…removed.

Tyler's throat was tight. His heart pulsed dully in his chest. Damon flicked the audio control.

"Good evening, Lucien," he said, his voice low and level. "No use pretending. I know you know we're here."

No reaction. Tyler lowered himself into a seat, unable to take his eyes from the haemophile but reluctant to be too close to Damon at the same time.

"I hope you enjoyed the show last night," Damon continued. Tyler looked at him. His expression was masked but a low light flickered in his silver eyes. "Perhaps if you answer some questions, we'll agree to a sequel."

Lucien still didn't move. Tyler fought a slump of disappointment.

Damon flicked the audio off again with a curse. "Stubborn. Figures."

"Do you really think he'll talk?"

"He'll talk," Damon said, pulling Lucien's file out of a drawer. He flicked the switch again. "Andrei Balan. Mariana Ungureanu. Luca Fischer. Remember them, Lucien?" Lucien didn't move. "They were your first three kills — or, at least, the first three we know about." Damon paused. Tyler fought the urge to shift in his seat. Still no reaction from the haemophile. "Maybe you don't remember them. Maybe they were too long ago.

Or maybe they weren't your first kills at all. Maybe there were dozens before them. Hundreds?"

Lucien finally opened his eyes. The unnerving redness made Tyler's stomach lurch at the same time as his blood stirred. They waited but he didn't speak. Damon clenched his jaw.

"They all died in Romania in the late sixteenth century," Damon continued, his voice flat, "in a small village in the Carpathian Mountains. The locals reported them as vampire attacks, but it was dismissed as peasant folklore." Lucien stared at them, unblinking. Tyler held himself very still. Damon's face hardened. "Is that where you're from, Lucien? Romania?"

*Nothing. Just that level, red stare – brighter than fresh blood, harder than rubies.*

"Do you remember killing these people? Drinking their blood? Leaving their bodies drained in their homes for their loved ones to find?"

Lucien's eyes moved from Damon to Tyler. Tyler stiffened. His palms were itching again, but his breathing was speeding up. The gaze lit something in him, low and dark and dangerous. He wanted more.

Damon made a noise and clicked the audio switch again. "As I suspected. This one's going to take time."

"How much time?"

"He's over five hundred years old," Damon said, gathering his papers. "He's used to things taking time. Well, this isn't my first rodeo. I can wait with the best of them." He turned to Tyler. "I'm heading out for some supplies. While I'm gone, see what you can get out of him."

"Wait! What do you mean?" Tyler said as Damon moved for the door.

"He knows you're here," Damon said, nodding at the haemophile. Tyler swallowed and looked around, but Lucien had closed his eyes again. "You intrigue him. See if he'll tell you something."

"Like what?"

"Anything," Damon said, opening the door. "Places he's lived. What dates he was in what countries. Where he's hidden the bodies that were never found. He's the oldest haemophile on record." Damon narrowed his eyes. The look in them was a tangled mix of curiosity and loathing. "He's bound to know something useful. How he's survived this long without going mad, for one. But, Tyler" — Damon looked him hard in the eyes — "stay on this side of the glass. Whatever he does, whatever he says…don't go in there. Okay?"

"You think I've got a death wish?"

"They can be very…persuasive. Just stay strong. I'll be back in a few hours. See if you can get him talking."

Damon closed the door behind him, and his footsteps faded to silence. Tyler turned back and started. Lucien had opened his eyes. He was looking right at him. Tyler swallowed. His breathing sounded loud in the still air. He glanced at the audio switch, but now that they were alone, all the hundreds of things he'd wanted to say had fled his brain.

"Stop pretending you can see me," he muttered through clenched teeth.

"I can see you."

Tyler started. Lucien's voice through the speakers wasn't loud, but it was like the room shook around him.

"No, you can't," Tyler stammered, checking the audio switch, still tuned to 'off'. "And you can't hear me, either."

"Of course I can."

Tyler shook his head. "This is a trick...to freak me out."

"Even if all this did work" — Lucien gestured at the glass with a long finger, his nails catching the light like claws — "your smell can't be kept out by walls, you know. Humans never understand how much scent gives away."

Tyler gripped the arms of the chair. "Why talk to me, huh? Damon's the one that wants to talk to you. I have no interest in anything you have to say."

"There's no point in lying to me," Lucien said softly.

Tyler stood. He opened and closed his fists, grinding his teeth. "Yeah, well, there's no point in you trying to fuck with my head anymore. I got you, you son of a bitch. You lost. I won."

Lucien got to his feet. His hair caught the light as it shifted, shimmering like ebony thread. His movements were almost boneless. He came up to the glass, and Tyler fought the urge to back away.

"You got me, as you say. I'm at your mercy. And yet here I am, still breathing, and you can't seem to stay away. What does that tell you?"

Tyler steadied his voice with an effort. "That I haven't decided the best way to make you pay."

Lucien seemed to search his face. "You're different from your friend," he said softly. "More conflicted but stronger."

"Are you gonna answer the question then?" Tyler bit out. "Who else have you killed?" He waved the list. "Who else belongs on this?"

Lucien tilted his head. "Have you actually read that list, Tyler?"

Tyler glanced at the paper then hurriedly set it aside. "I know it's long. That's all that matters."

"It's more than that. And you, unlike your friend, have the capacity to understand it. Understand *me*."

Tyler's skin flooded with heat. His body began to shake as Lucien continued to gaze at him, less than three feet away, walled behind glass.

"Why did you want me to watch, Tyler?" Lucien asked softly. His voice had changed. Lowered, grown warm. "Why did you want me to watch you having sex?"

Tyler's dick twitched, even though his skin chilled. "Don't mean anything," he said. "I get off on being watched. That's it."

"If you really loathed me like you claim," Lucien said after a long silence, "having me watch wouldn't excite you."

"You liked it, too," Tyler snapped. "That blank face doesn't fool me. You liked watching, so don't pretend you didn't. You didn't even blink."

"I did like it," Lucien said softly. "I liked it very much."

Tyler stilled. Words left him.

"It surprises me as much as it surprises you," Lucien continued. "It's been many years since I've felt that kind of stimulation. I can't claim to understand it, but there's no use denying it. Like you say…you could tell."

"Stop fucking with my head."

"I'm not."

Tyler clenched his fists. "You get off on killing people. No way you'd turn me on."

Lucien stared at him. "Read the list again, Tyler. Follow your instincts. Then try being more honest with yourself."

Tyler made a noise of frustration. "Shut up, will you? Just shut up. Or I'll turn those day-floods on."

"I'd appreciate it if you didn't."

Tyler shifted on his feet, glanced at the wall of weapons and away again.

"Yes," Lucien said, following his glance. "You know the truth about your friend. That's yet another thing you need to be honest with yourself about."

"He gets that you're a killer—that people need to be protected from you."

"You really think Terry Fleetwood deserved protection?"

Tyler's chest tightened. Something in Lucien's gaze had changed. It made Tyler's heart skip about in his chest.

"You attacked me. You called me weak. You would have killed me if Magnusson hadn't stopped you."

"And yet you've hunted for me ever since…knowing how easily I could end your life."

Tyler shifted on his feet. The back of his neck tingled.

Lucien leaned forward. He gazed up at Tyler through his lashes. "Do you want to see my body, Tyler?"

"Wha…what?"

Lucien tilted his head. His eyes danced. "Humans are obsessed with the physical. The aesthetic. And our metabolism gifts us certain advantages in that area."

"You sure think a lot of yourself."

"So you don't want to see?" Tyler clenched his mouth shut. Lucien didn't look away. "If you ask, I'll show you."

"I told you to stop fucking with me."

"And I told you that I'm not," Lucien said, lifting a hand and running a finger down the glass. "You're in control here, Tyler. I'll give you what you want…if you admit you want it."

"So now you wanna get off on messing with me?"

"I'm stimulated by you," he said, so softly the mics barely picked it up. "But I'm not interested in fulfilling any desires you are ashamed of."

"Why me?" Tyler croaked after a long silence. "Why are you interested in me? You wanted to kill me. You said so."

Lucien ran his finger back up the glass, slowly, leaning so close his breath misted across its surface. His eyes were unblinking, glowing like shards of ruby under moonlight. His lips were parted, his mouth red and wet. Tyler was painfully hard. But he kept his hands clenched at his sides.

"You understand," Lucien breathed.

Tyler sucked in air, willing it to douse his arousal, but the haemophile's unblinking gaze only made it hotter.

"What do you want, Tyler?" Lucien whispered.

Tyler couldn't tell if he were intentionally echoing Damon's question, but either way, somehow, he knew Lucien already knew the answer.

"You have to tell me," Lucien said as if in answer to his thought. "Tell yourself."

"I want to see you…" He clamped his mouth shut.

"See me what?"

Tyler swallowed. When he spoke, his voice was hoarse. "See you. All of you."

Lucien didn't smile but something brightened in his jewel-like eyes. "You would enjoy that? Seeing me disrobe?"

"Call it stripping, for fuck's sake," Tyler bit out. "We're not in some Victorian burlesque whatever."

"No. Though that's a shame. I think you might have enjoyed some of the ones I visited in my time." Tyler's throat closed over, and Lucien's eyes flickered. He tilted his head again. "Okay, Tyler. We'll use your words. Would you like me to strip for you?"

Tyler nodded stiffly, biting his lip so hard it hurt.

"As you wish."

Lucien shrugged off his long, black coat. He folded it neatly and laid it on top of his sleeping cell. Next he pulled off his jumper. His hair fell around his face, but he didn't break eye contact. His mouth was open. Tyler caught a glimpse of his teeth and inhaled sharply. Lucien let the jumper dangle from one finger, then dropped it to the floor. Slowly, he started unbuttoning his shirt. Tyler forced himself to keep his hands away from his belt. He knew the second he touched himself he would explode. He wanted this to last. Any inner voice telling him why he shouldn't want it at all had fallen silent the second Lucien had run his finger down the glass.

It seemed to take Lucien an age to unfasten his shirt. Tyler silently marveled at the way his fingers dealt with the buttons with such long nails. He caught glimpses of smooth, hairless skin, and his heart began to pound.

Lucien watched Tyler intently as he shrugged his shirt from his shoulders. Tyler couldn't suppress a low noise. Lucien was as slim as a dancer, as toned as an athlete. His chest was smooth, his pecs as unblemished as marble. His nipples were dusky pink. His shoulders rolled with his movements, the muscles rippling as he finished removing the shirt and let it fall to the ground. His stomach was as ridged as a swimmer's. His arms were slim and very long. They would have looked odd on a human, but with his overly perfect physique, it was visually stunning.

Tyler trembled to think of the strength in those arms that he'd felt out on the moor, incapacitating him. A strength that had almost ended him. Now those same hands were moving toward the fastening of his trousers, and Lucien was staring at him with hot, red eyes.

"Do you like what you see?"

Tyler nodded dumbly, his face filling with heat, his groin pulsing like an extra heartbeat.

"Tell me what you're feeling…" There was a hint of urgency in Lucien's tone. The sound sent ripples through Tyler's flesh.

"Christ," he managed, voice hoarse. "I feel like I'm about to burst."

"Describe it to me," Lucien breathed, his chest swelling with his increasing breath. "Every detail."

"My skin is hot," he said. "My legs are shaking. I'm so fucking hard it hurts. Keep going."

The corner of a smile twitched Lucien's lips. Tyler made a low noise. Maddeningly slowly, Lucien stripped off the remainder of his clothing. He straightened. He stood, naked and glorious. His legs were as toned as the rest of him, dusted with dark hair. There was more dark hair gathered at his crotch. His hands were at his sides, and his eyes were locked on Tyler. Tyler groaned aloud and yanked his jeans open with a gasp of relief. He began to stroke himself, roaming his eyes over Lucien's body, grabbing the desk for support. He drank in the sight, the gorgeous body, the bewitching eyes, his perfect skin that Tyler suddenly would have given anything, even his life, to touch.

He stopped, blinking until his eyes focused again. "You're not hard," he said, a chill threatening to damp the heat riding through him.

"Tell me what you're feeling," Lucien said softly.

Tyler tugged himself lightly, breathing deep. "Touch yourself, and you'll know."

"It's different for us," Lucien said, though his eyes lowered to Tyler's hand on his dick. "And it's been a long time for me. Remind me what it feels like. Tell me how good you feel."

"It's like fire and ice together," Tyler forced the words out, even though his tongue felt thick and heavy in his mouth. "It burns. Throbs. I can't even... It's building in here," Tyler clutched his lower belly with his free hand. "And in here." He laid his hand on his chest. "But mostly here," he said, kneading his balls with his free hand as he pumped himself with the other. "Please. Touch yourself. I wanna see you touch yourself."

"Finally...some honesty."

The heat in Lucien's eyes took all the harshness from his words. Tyler stilled his hands. Lucien ran one of his own over his chest, down his toned stomach, then lower. Tyler held his breath, then released a low groan of desperation as Lucien took a gentle hold of his dick. Tyler raised his eyes to the haemophile's face with a monumental effort. Lucien locked gazes with him and started to stroke himself—long, slow, controlled strokes that had Tyler's balls clenching.

He suddenly longed more than anything to have those hands on his body, on his cock, stroking it in that same slow, deliberate rhythm, coaxing out a desire in him so deep-rooted and colossal that it scared him a little.

"Tell me, Tyler," Lucien whispered. The huskiness in his voice made Tyler's knees weaken. "Tell me what you'd do if this glass wasn't here."

"Fuck," Tyler started working himself again. "Move faster. Make yourself so hard it aches."

Lucien obeyed, and soon his eyes hooded and his mouth opened wider. He put a hand against the glass to hold himself up. Tyler could see his limbs tremble as his strokes gained urgency. His eyes fluttered shut, and his bottom lip glistened with saliva. Tyler had to bite his own to stop from coming at the sight. Lucien pumped himself faster, his cock flushed and stiffened in his hands and Tyler's entire body shook.

"Now *you* tell *me* what you're feeling," he breathed.

Lucien opened his eyes. They were blazing. His breathing was ragged. "I feel like I need something," he said, his voice harsh and low. "Need more than what I can give myself."

"Imagine it's me," Tyler ordered, working his own cock. Lightning started to gather under his abdomen. "Imagine that's my hand on you. Imagine what I could do, how hard I could make you come."

"I'm already imagining that," he breathed. "I'm picturing every detail. Are you?"

Tyler came, fast and hot. His sight went...then his knees. His body was washed through head to foot with ecstasy. Time reeled away — then the world, then even the memory that there once existed something called pain.

When his focus finally returned, he was slumped bonelessly in Damon's chair. His hand and jeans were sticky.

Lucien still had his hand against the glass. Condensation gathered under his palm and from his heavy breath. Tyler leaned forward to see the visual evidence that he, too, had climaxed. His throat closed to see the wetness glistening on Lucien's hand and softening cock.

A lazy thrill quivered through his body at the sight.

Lucien raised his eyes. They stared at each other. Then Lucien turned away and started to dress. Tyler frowned. Lucien's breathing had already returned to normal. The color had left his face. All traces of sated desire had evaporated from his eyes.

"That's it?"

Lucien didn't look at him. He returned to his spot against the wall and sat, folding his hands in his lap.

"Hey," Tyler barked, banging the glass. "You can't just do that then pretend nothing happened."

"I'm still your prisoner," Lucien said without opening his eyes. "I can't pretend that that isn't happening, either."

"Fuck you," Tyler said, tucking himself away and fastening his jeans. "You said you weren't fucking with me. You were totally fucking with me."

"Read the list, Tyler. Decide what you want. Then we can talk more."

Tyler grabbed the file and shook it at the glass.

"You bet I'm gonna read it. Remind myself why you deserve to be in there. Deserve everything you've got coming to you."

He slammed out of the observation room. When he reached the living quarters, he slapped the file onto the desk. He hovered, rubbing his mouth and glaring at it. Then he sat and opened it.

*He's still a monster. No matter how fuckable he is.*

Damon's words circled in his head, drowning out his sister's warnings, drowning out his own thoughts and the dull, gray pain of his disappointment.

He made himself take in the injury details of the men left outside Fulford Road station. He read the collection of articles of other, unsolved attacks and murders Damon had collected. Then, finally, he turned again to the Kill List. His belly dipped. If Damon was right, this was only some of the story. There were names unlisted. Souls unmourned. Bodies undiscovered.

Desire drained out of him as he read. Different races, ages, countries, centuries. His chest tightened until he got to the 1900s again and stopped. Again, one name jumped out at him.

*Francis Tumblety, 1903, St. Louis, USA.*

Tyler chewed the inside of his cheek, something tickling at his memory. He pulled out his phone and googled the name.

He stared at his screen for a long time, not wanting to admit to the realization. He picked other names from the list to search. Most came up with no hits at all. One or two of the more recent ones had articles on Wikipedia or news archive websites. They ranged from three-line obituaries in the local paper to headline reports of high-profile deaths. Nothing appeared to link them, not even geography.

Apart from the more he searched, the more Tyler saw a picture building. Names linked to other names, places, businesses that had ended up in the news long after the person's demise for all the wrong reasons.

He started when he heard the sound of footsteps approaching. Damon opened the door. He was wearing a wide, unseemly smile.

"So you got him to admit he wants to fuck you," he said as he came in and put a small bag on the sofa. "That's a very promising start."

Tyler blinked, heat flooding his face. "What?"

Damon jerked a thumb at the door. "That was a good performance. Got right under his skin. And that's some mighty fine skin, don't you think?"

"How...? How do you know?"

Damon gave him an odd look. "There are cameras everywhere, remember?"

Tyler flushed hot. "You taped us?"

Damon chuckled and sat. "Don't come over all shy, Tyler. I don't care how we get results, so long as we get them. And you're clearly better at getting them from him than I am." He grinned again and began unloading metal flasks from the bag, then a glass vial.

"What's that?"

"Food. For our guest." He tapped the vial. "With a little something to keep him under control."

"Drugs?"

Damon frowned at his tone as he unscrewed the first flask. "You might have got him horny, but he'd still rip your throat out, given half the chance. If you want to get close enough to finish him, we need to start building this up in his system."

"I..." Tyler couldn't make the words come out. Damon frowned harder. "I don't think we should."

Damon set the vial aside. "Should what?"

"Finish him."

Damon stared at him. The impish joviality had gone from his eyes. "Look... Having cold feet is under-standable—"

"It's not cold feet."

"Then what?"

Tyler picked at a loose fingernail. "I... I don't think we've understood this."

"Of course we have," Damon said levelly. "He's a killer. He almost killed *you*. Still would, if he could."

"I don't know about that anymore."

"I told you not to listen to him, Tyler," Damon said after a loaded silence. "He's trying to manipulate you. It's okay to want him." Damon said, raising a hand to cut off Tyler's protests. "Christ knows I've wanted to do all sorts in the past. But never forget what he is."

"Damon," Tyler said, holding out the list. "Do you know who's on this list?"

"People," Daron said, not taking the paper. "Hundreds of them. People whose lives *he* ended."

"Francis Tumblety," Tyler insisted, tapping the name. "You know who he is, right?"

"He was some quack American doctor," Damon said, unscrewing another flask. "A misogynist and an arsehole by all accounts. He still didn't deserve to be murdered."

"He was a Jack the Ripper suspect," Tyler said, sitting on the sofa and thrusting his phone with the article at Damon. "In London at the time of all the canonical murders. Hated women. Mad as toast."

"Tyler—"

"It was him, Damon," Tyler insisted, shaking the phone. "He was Jack the Ripper."

"Jesus, Tyler. Really? You're really going there?"

"This Tumblety brutally murdered at least five women, probably more. Are you still saying he didn't deserve what Lucien did to him?"

"Lucien doesn't discriminate," Damon said calmly, pushing his phone back to him. "So he happened to kill one person who could well have been a murdering psychopath. Does that rid him of the guilt of all the others?"

"But I think the others are pieces of work, too." Tyler shook the paper. "I've found pedophile politicians, abusive parents, corrupt business owners. I bet every name on this list belongs to someone twisted."

"I've been through that list hundreds of times," Damon said, treating the last flask without making eye contact. "Some of them have sketchy histories, sure, but most don't have any history at all. Just poor souls that crossed his path when he was hungry."

"You're not listening."

"I am," Damon said, gathering the flasks and standing. "Even if you were right—and that's a big 'if', Tyler—who gave Lucien the right to do this? Who appointed him judge, jury and executioner of the human race?" He turned his back and went to the door. "I'm going to give our guest his dinner. I suggest you use the time to get your head back in the game."

"He won't eat it," Tyler said, hoping it was true. "He can fucking smell us through a concrete wall. He'll be able to smell if you've drugged his blood."

"Let me worry about that," Damon said as he opened the door. "You concentrate on forgetting everything he's managed to make you believe because he gave you a flash of skin."

Damon didn't come near Tyler that night. He sat working on his computer and drinking coffee, his face a mask of intent. Tyler dozed fitfully on top of the covers, alternating between staring at the wall in the light of Damon's computer screen to struggling with confusing dreams that were both appealing and terrifying.

He must have finally drifted off, because the sound of Damon locking the door woke him some hours later. His watch told him it was getting on to nine a.m. He frowned at the locked door, his sleep-deprived brain taking a while to process.

He scrambled out of bed and grabbed the handle. It rattled but the door didn't budge. He kicked it, swore again then spotted the note next to the kettle.

*It's for your own good. Back later.*

Tyler stood in the middle of the strange, windowless room with unease thrumming every nerve in his body.

The day crawled by. He turned on the TV, surfed the web, trying to find more evidence to convince Damon he wasn't crazy. But his mind wouldn't settle on any one thing. He was too full of anger, nervousness and an intense impatience for nightfall for another chance to see Lucien — to see him touch himself again, to hear him breathe Tyler's name in that low, intimate voice.

He jerked off in the bathroom whenever it became too much, but each climax felt dim.

When the day finally began to give way to night, he heard footsteps in the corridor. He launched himself at the door the second Damon opened it. But Damon, quicker than a snake, drew a knife. Tyler wheeled to a stop. Damon stood frozen, his eyes hard, the knife steady between them.

"I'd hoped it wouldn't come to this, Tyler."

"You locked me in."

"I know you understand this is all for a good reason. Now, can I put this knife away?"

"Are you gonna let me go?"

"Go where? You can't leave the compound without a car. And, for tonight, I think it's best you avoid the observation room, too."

"What? Why?"

"I think he may be ready to answer some questions," Damon said, still watching him like a cat watching a mouse as he sheathed the knife. "You being there would muddy the waters."

"You're the one who said I got him loosened up…"

"You have. But tonight, I think it would be best just me and him. See how much he'll give me, knowing he might get the chance to see you again. Now are you going to be a good boy and stay put? Or am I going to have to lock you in again?"

"Are you gonna hurt him?" Tyler said, surprising himself with the emotion in his voice.

Damon studied him, then looked away. "I don't think we're there yet. Besides, you catch more flies with honey. Here." He held out a shopping bag that clinked. Tyler took it numbly. There was a frozen pizza, beer and crisps. "Entertain yourself for a few hours. Then maybe I'll see what I can do to entertain you later." His smile turned suggestive. Tyler couldn't find a reply or decide how he felt about that.

Thankfully, Damon didn't seem to notice. He left the room. Tyler listened for the lock but only heard Damon's footsteps fading away. He went to the door. It opened. The corridor beyond was empty. He almost ran but then he caught the blinking eye of the camera in the corridor. He retreated and slumped on the couch. He stared at the TV…and the camera on top.

Damon returned a couple of hours later. He was smiling in that way Tyler was starting to dislike.

"What happened?"

"Nothing you need to concern yourself with. But I have to go out."

"What? Where?"

"I just have to confirm some things. You should stay here."

"I'm not letting you lock me in again—"

Damon raised his hands. "I won't lock you in. You're not a prisoner, Tyler. But I am locking the observation room. It's best you keep away from him tonight."

"*Why?*"

Damon's smile never wavered. "He'll be more pliable if you play hard to get. Don't worry. I've got something extra special planned for tomorrow."

He left. Tyler stared at the open doorway in a confused daze until he heard the lift doors close. Then he shook himself and stalked out of the room, ignoring the cameras. He rattled the locked door to the observation room with a curse then backtracked to the cell door itself, but that, too, of course, was locked. He pressed his hand to the cold steel, imagining he could feel Lucien's presence on the other side. He wondered if Damon had drugged him…or worse.

He hurried away before the thoughts could fully form.

He grabbed his phone off the bed. He brought up his sister's contact info and his thumb hovered over the call button.

*What would I say?*

He slumped on the bed and put his head in his hands.

"Tyler?"

Tyler jerked up. Lucien stood in the doorway.

# Chapter Six

Lucien was leaning on the doorframe. His eyes were clouded. His skin was a sickly shade of gray.

Tyler's heart began to pound, but whether it was excitement or terror he couldn't decide.

"You need to leave." Lucien's voice was thick. Sluggish. "Now."

Tyler stood uneasily. "How did you get out?"

"Tyler, you have to go." His legs buckled, and he clung to the doorframe.

Tyler frowned. "Did you drink that drugged blood?"

Lucien nodded, took a shaky step into the room and collapsed against the wall. He raised his head with what looked like a great effort. "It'll be easier this way."

"What will?"

"Tyler," he said again, staring hard at him, "he's going to hurt you."

"What?"

"That man. He's going to torture you. He's going to make me watch." Lucien nodded at the camera over the TV.

Tyler opened and closed his fists, fighting understanding, fighting the powerful urge to go to him. "You're lying."

Lucien closed his eyes and leaned his head against the wall. "He thinks it will make me tell him more. And he's probably right. Please, Tyler. I don't care what he finds out about me, but I can't tell him our secrets...'my kind's' secrets."

Tyler was hot and cold all over. "Why would I make any difference?"

Lucien tried to straighten from the wall and staggered. Tyler rushed forward and caught him. He was a lot heavier than Tyler was expecting. The smell of his hair and skin surrounded Tyler, dizzying him. Tyler's heart slugged against his ribs. Lucien raised his head.

"Tyler," he murmured. "*Please.*"

"I don't get it," Tyler said, his voice catching. "If you could escape this whole time...why did you stay?"

"Tyler..."

"Tell me."

Lucien's knees buckled. Tyler helped him to the bed. He sat on the edge with his head hanging. His silk-fine hair hung around him, hiding his face. Tyler went to the fridge, found a blood flask and brought it over.

"Here. This stuff's fresh. Will it help?"

"I don't want it."

"Come on," Tyler said impatiently, ignoring the circling fear in his gut and unscrewing the flask. "You're about to keel over. Here."

He held the flask out. Lucien inhaled deeply. He straightened. His eyes had changed. The muscles in his jaw and neck were taught. He snatched the flask and drank deeply, closing his eyes.

Tyler looked away and tried to ignore the coppery smell. When he turned back, Lucien was sitting straighter, and his eyes were brighter.

"I didn't want that," he said softly. "I only came out here to warn you."

"Why haven't you *run*?" Tyler demanded.

Lucien held his gaze, unflinching. "Perhaps this is what I want."

"You want Damon to kill you? 'Cause that's what he's working up to, trust me." Lucien just stared at him. Tyler scowled. "You're jerking me around again."

"I'm not."

"You're not telling me you *want* to die. That's bullshit."

"Of course I don't want to die. But at this point, there is no other way."

"No other way to what?"

Lucien looked at the wall. "To be free of all this. For this to be over."

"What are you on about?"

Lucien raised his eyes. "I don't belong to this world anymore. It doesn't want me in it. It can't handle what I do. Even you wanted me gone. And you're the first human I've met in centuries who..." He lowered his gaze. "Even *you* wanted me gone."

Tyler blinked, mind reeling, then scowled. "That was before."

"Before what?"

Tyler ground his teeth. "I dunno. Before whatever this... Look...just stop killing people. That would solve everything."

"It's not that simple."

Tyler made an impatient gesture. "Sure it is. Get registered. Play by the new rules, like everyone else. Plenty of haemos get by without killing anyone—or so they say. Or is that really all just a cover like people have told me?"

"Others have found ways to change," Lucien said quietly. "To integrate. But I'm too old. Too different. I can't change my nature any more than you could."

"What's that supposed to mean?"

Lucien observed him in silence for a long moment. "Are you telling me you wouldn't have assaulted your friend's husband if you'd known what he was doing to her?"

Tyler stared. "How do you know I know Charlene?"

"I know a lot about you, Tyler…and this city. I make it my business to know these things. And you didn't answer my question." His eyes flashed. "If you'd known that man was abusing her, would you have left him unpunished?"

Tyler opened and closed his fists again. His skin felt hot. "That's different."

"How?"

"I don't kill people. I never would."

"These people…" He nodded to where his file lay open on the desk. "They needed to die."

Tyler shifted on his feet, trying to filter all the responses clamoring in his head. "The four scumbags you dumped on those steps. They were all still breathing."

"I decided to give your justice system a chance, the way you did." His eyes hardened. "But if it fails their victims—which is likely—I will know. And next time there would be no visit to the police station."

"You *didn't* kill them," Tyler insisted. "You *chose* not to. So you do have a choice."

Lucien frowned thoughtfully. "You brought me here to kill me, Tyler. I know you were conflicted about it. But it still means that you know, deep down, sometimes there is only one way to solve these things."

Tyler scowled at the wall.

Lucien stood. He took an unsteady step closer. "This is as it should be, Tyler. I want to be at peace. I just have one thing to make right before that happens."

Tyler looked into his face. He swallowed. "What?"

Lucien lifted his hands. They hovered over Tyler's arms but didn't touch. "I made you afraid to touch people. To be touched. For that I'm sorry. I would like to fix that, if you'll let me."

"I... I don't know what you..."

Lucien leaned close and ghosted his lips over Tyler's. Tyler shivered. The touch was electric. Fire danced along his nerves. His whole body stiffened. Lucien ran his hands up his arms, strong but gentle. He tilted his head to run his tongue over Tyler's lips. Instead of wanting to back away, all Tyler wanted was more, but his limbs were like lead.

"I'll give you what you need, Tyler," Lucien whispered against his lips as he ran his fingers over to his neck. His skin was cool. His fingers were long and strong, but they brushed Tyler's skin so lightly it was like the touch of feathers. "I'll help you feel like you again."

Tyler growled, grabbed Lucien's arms and shoved him onto the bed. He climbed on top and captured his mouth. Lucien made a low noise and dug his fingers into Tyler's lower back, crushing them together.

"You don't scare me, Lucien," Tyler growled into his mouth. "And you don't fool me, either."

"I'm not trying to fool you…" Lucien cut off with a gasp as Tyler mouthed at the tender skin under his ear. He tasted like rich wine and winter bonfires, dark chocolate and strong liquor. Tyler was dizzy with all of it but continued to lavish attention on Lucien's neck while running his hands all over what parts of his body he could reach.

"You're pretending this is all for me," Tyler mumbled against Lucien's skin. "But you need something, too. Something real. Something different."

Lucien rolled Tyler under him and straddled his hips. His eyes were lit from within. His lips were wet and parted, and color rode high on his cheeks. Tyler thought he might come just from the sight, but Lucien bent over and brushed his lips all over Tyler's face, kissing his eyes, his cheeks, his chin.

"You're beautiful, Tyler," Lucien whispered. "Forged in fire. Welded like steel. Just like me."

"I want to see you again," Tyler said, pulling at Lucien's clothes, his cock already aching. Lucien pulled off his jumper and shirt in one motion. Tyler breathed deep, momentarily paralyzed. Then he lifted shaking hands to brush his fingers over Lucien's abdomen. It was unnervingly cool, so smooth it was like velvet, even though the muscles beneath were harder than iron.

"This is what I wanted," he said, his voice trembling, the words spilling out from a dark, secret place inside him. "This is what I needed, all this time."

"You don't need to be afraid of what you want," Lucien whispered, taking one of Tyler's hands and guiding it up his chest to his neck. "Not anymore."

"I'm not afraid," Tyler lied and made himself meet Lucien's unnerving gaze.

Lucien smiled. "Your hands are very warm. It feels good."

Tyler's confidence swelled. He ran his hands down Lucien's chest and stomach, swallowing as he reached his waistband. He pressed his palm against Lucien's crotch but found no answering hardness there. He swallowed. "Not good enough?"

"Relax," Lucien said, lifting Tyler's hand in his mouth and brushing his lips over his knuckles. "This is about you."

Tyler was about to protest when Lucien undid his belt. He gasped as his erection was freed. Lucien pushed Tyler's shirt to his chest and brushed more kisses over his belly.

"I will do this for you," he whispered against his skin as his long fingers trailed up and down Tyler's thighs, slowly driving him mad. "Then you have to leave. Understand?"

"Lucien…"

Lucien froze, his mouth hovering over Tyler's swollen cock, his eyes locked on Tyler's. "Promise, Tyler. You have to promise you'll leave."

"Fuck, yes, I promise," Tyler said, arching off the bed in desperation. "Please, God, just…"

Lucien's face relaxed, and he lowered his head. He took Tyler all the way into his mouth and into his throat in one smooth movement. Tyler bucked and swore. The tight, wet heat was too much. He fisted the bedclothes and groaned out loud. Lucien lifted his head, running his tongue along the underside of Tyler's cock and swirled it around the head.

White light fired along Tyler's limbs. He forced his eyes open to watch as Lucien took him all the way in again. It was so good, so easy. Lucien's touch reached parts of him he hadn't even acknowledged in months. His skin was still raw, like a healing wound, but Lucien's contact was soothing, a cooling balm.

But it wasn't enough. He wanted to see what Lucien looked like when he was made to feel this way…when something drove him to a point where there was barely any control left, where nothing existed but the sensations, the pleasure, the intensity.

He opened his mouth to say something, but then Lucien swallowed him again and cupped his balls with his free hand. He kneaded them tenderly and hummed around Tyler's cock.

The world fragmented into glittering points of light. He came hard and fast, riding a wave of fire. He arched off the bed, thrusting deep into Lucien's mouth, dizzy and aching with the intensity of the release.

When he had regained enough strength to raise his head, Lucien was still sitting across his thighs. He was running those long hands up and down his hips and legs, looking down at him with hooded eyes.

"I think with your next lover, you will be able to do more than just watch."

Tyler sat up, thrust his fingers into Lucien's hair and pulled his head down. He crushed their mouths together. He swept his tongue into that rich, hot mouth, tasting himself on Lucien's tongue and shivering. Lucien responded with a low noise, swirling his tongue over Tyler's, seemingly breathing his scent in deep.

Tyler broke away to breathe and locked eyes with him. "I don't want anyone else."

"This is far as we go," Lucien said softly, taking Tyler's hands and lowering them. "Remember your promise."

Tyler grabbed Lucien's wrist to stop him from pulling away. "We're not done."

Lucien gave him a level look. "You know you can't hold me."

"You need more," he said. "I can give you what you need, too. I know I can."

Lucien swallowed. The sight of the muscles in his neck moving made Tyler start to harden again. "There's no time."

"I don't care."

"*I* care, Tyler," Lucien insisted, pulling his wrist from Tyler's grip and standing. "And you need to leave."

"I will. I'll keep my promise…" He took a deep breath, feeling like he was perched on a soap bubble. "Come with me."

Lucien frowned. "I'm sorry?"

"Come with me," he repeated, more insistently.

Lucien shook his head. "That's not how this is supposed to go."

"Fuck 'supposed to' anything," Tyler said, standing and pulling on his trousers. "We're going. Together. *Now*."

"I can't," he said as he pulled his own jumper back on. "There's nothing for me out there."

"What about me?"

Lucien gave him a pained look. "Tyler — "

"We're going," Tyler said and grabbed his hand. "*Now*."

To Tyler's secret relief and astonishment, Lucien allowed himself to be dragged to the lift. He was still unsteady on his feet. Tyler had to hold him under the elbow. Tyler jabbed the button. Lucien tilted his head, like he was listening.

"He's close."

"Damon?" Tyler blanched. "How close?" Lucien didn't answer. "Lucien, get in."

Tyler fought the urge to drag him into the lift. Finally, Lucien stepped inside. Tyler let out the breath he'd been holding and pressed the button.

The upstairs room was deserted. Tyler went straight to the door and jerked the handle, but it was locked. He swore and kicked it. "That bastard," he said.

"Here," Lucien said, stepping past him and twisting the handle. There was a groan of protesting metal. The handle snapped and the door swung open. In blew the warm night air, heavy with the smells of leaf mold and distant woodsmoke.

"Come on," Tyler said, grabbing Lucien's hand and pulling him out into the night. He started to head for the track, but Lucien steered him the other way.

"He's too close. This way."

Lucien took them into the scattered moonlight below the trees. Tyler's heart leapt into his throat when he heard an engine in the distance.

"Hurry," Lucien said, pulling Tyler until they were running. Tyler stumbled on roots and fallen branches, but Lucien caught him every time. They stopped at a gate. Lucien appeared on the other side without having apparently made a move. Tyler followed, more ungainly, then they were running again, across an open field.

"Where are we going?" Tyler panted, but then Lucien grabbed him and shoved him flat on the ground. Over his pounding heart, Tyler made out the sound of a vehicle approaching. Headlights swept over the trees ahead of them. Through a gap in a nearby wall, Tyler caught a glimpse of the road. Damon's van crawled by. Lucien didn't move until both the sight and sound of it had been swallowed into the night.

"He won't let us go easy," Tyler said.

"I know somewhere," Lucien murmured. "Somewhere he won't find us."

"What are we waiting for?"

Lucien was regarding him levelly in the moonlight. The silvery illumination shone off his cheekbones and hair. The deep red of his eyes appeared to glow in the darkness. Tyler couldn't tell if he wanted to run as fast as he could back to Damon or push Lucien into the leaves and kiss him until he couldn't breathe.

"If I take you to this place, you have to swear to never reveal its location to anyone...*ever*."

Tyler frowned. "What? Why?"

"It's a secret bolthole. Somewhere safe my kind can go when they need to hide."

Tyler knew a flare of his old anger. "An unregistered hide?"

It was a moment before Lucien answered. "That's not what we call them."

"Why do you need these secret places, Lucien? They seem to cause nothing but trouble."

"Innocent and guilty isn't as simple as left and right, Tyler. Look at you and me."

"Our kinds can never trust each other if you keep secrets like this."

"We wouldn't do it if we didn't need to. Damon's not alone in his attitudes, you know. Far from it. You shared them yourself."

Tyler looked away, grinding his teeth. "Okay. Maybe I get that."

"You 'get' more than you think you do," Lucien said, drawing Tyler to his feet. "You, too, need somewhere safe right now, yes? Well…"

"I promise I won't tell anyone."

"Don't promise, Tyler. Swear…on whatever it is you're feeling for me, on this thing that you can't let go that's been ruling your dreams since we met. Swear on that. I know it will hold you to your word."

Tyler gazed into his wide, burning eyes. His throat threatened to close over. "I swear, Lucien."

It was another breathless moment before Lucien moved. But, finally, he nodded, turned and drew Tyler along the wall, away from the road. They moved fast, jogging or running, Lucien helping Tyler over walls, fences and hedges. They ran for what felt like hours. Tyler tried to figure out what he was doing the whole time and couldn't.

Dawn began to silver the eastern horizon. Tyler could make out more detail of the countryside around them—the rocks in the field boundary walls, the crowded little copse ahead. Lucien staggered. His shoulders were rigid. Tyler reached out for him, but Lucien pushed him away.

"Don't touch me right now," he whispered. "It's not safe." Fear flickered under Tyler's skin as he noted the set look on Lucien's face. "Don't worry," he rasped. "We're almost there."

They moved into the lingering darkness under the trees, and Lucien appeared to ease. They waded through bracken and brambles until they reached what looked like a derelict electric substation.

Lucien tapped a code into the keypad on the door of the small, concrete building and opened it. Inside it was utterly dark and smelled damp. Tyler wrinkled his nose. "This is where you want to sleep?"

He jumped when Lucien curled his fingers through his in the darkness. "This way," he said and guided Tyler into the shadows. "Step down."

Tyler put his foot out onto nothing and stumbled. But Lucien eased him forward and he found a step. Then another. It was so dark it didn't make any difference whether Tyler had his eyes open or shut. The temperature dropped rapidly.

When he heard the sound of a door clicking shut over his head, Tyler's chest started to constrict. But then Lucien's gentle touch was running down his arms.

"I won't let you fall," he said. "Keep walking."

Tyler continued down the unseen steps. Finally, he was on level ground. Lucien slipped away, and Tyler stood in the darkness with his heart hammering against his ribs.

There was another click, and a sudden light made Tyler blink.

Tyler stared around him in amazement. He was in what looked like a well-appointed living room. There was a sofa against the wall, a fridge in the corner next to a small sink. There was a bookshelf full of books, and there were magazines on a coffee table. The walls were plastered and painted a pleasant terracotta. The lamp Lucien had just turned on stood on the coffee table and flooded the space in a warm, low light. It looked like a completely ordinary room, apart from the lack of windows and the large sleeping cell against the opposite wall.

"The place in York wasn't like this."

"That one is only supposed to be for those passing through. Ones like this can sustain us for as long as we need."

"It's not what I was expecting," Tyler said, shifting uncomfortably.

"Would you prefer we slept in tombs and crypts?" Lucien said with a half-smile as he moved over to the sleeping cell. "We did, once," he said as he lifted the lid. "The only way we were guaranteed peace…and darkness. It's how some of the stories started. But the world has moved on."

He turned and looked at Tyler. His eyes were heavy. "The sun is rising. I need to sleep." Tyler nodded awkwardly, rubbing his eyes. He was suddenly so exhausted it almost hurt.

"Yeah, okay. I can hang out here, I guess."

"You're tired, Tyler. You should sleep, too."

Tyler snorted. "Not much chance of that," he said, looking around the strange room, rubbing his arms, still feeling unpleasantly closed in.

Lucien held his hand out. "You can sleep with me if you want."

Tyler stared. "I can?"

"I think I can help you sleep. Help you feel safe."

Tyler stared at the open sleeping cell. It looked big enough for two, but still…

"I thought it was really dangerous to be around you guys when you're sleeping?"

"Only if you try to wake me. But you'll sleep through, I think. And this way I can protect us both."

Tyler shivered. But the look in Lucien's eyes was warm and receptive. He still held his hand out.

Tyler took it. Lucien drew him close. He brushed kisses over his eyebrows, cheeks and lips. "I don't understand this, Tyler," he breathed. "I'm so tired. I'm so scared. Have been for years... But you seem to ease all that."

"I do?" His blood was stirring as Lucien's sleepy embrace wrapped around him.

Lucien nodded and drew him close. "Come. Let's rest."

They climbed into the cell. Tyler was surprised to find the interior lined in soft padding and some kind of silky fabric. Lucien drew him down, so they were lying on their sides. He gathered Tyler close, and Tyler allowed himself to be drawn in and wrapped in his arms. When Lucien closed the lid, they were plunged into utter darkness. For a second it was all too much— the dark, the narrow space, another body so close, holding him still. But Lucien was so firm, so strong and smelled so good, that Tyler's muscles quickly eased. He rested his head against Lucien's shoulder, breathed in the smell of his hair and started to drift.

Lucien's breathing slowed until the point where it almost stopped. But the gentle hold he had on Tyler didn't loosen. Tyler allowed himself to let go.

He didn't dream. He didn't wake up screaming. He didn't even wake up to adjust position or turn over in Lucien's arms.

He slept so deeply that when Lucien stirred, it took Tyler several moments to figure out where he was. The memories came flooding back. He felt Lucien's body slowly coming to life beside him and heard him take a deep, sighing breath.

Tyler was instantly hard. He groped for Lucien's mouth in the darkness, found it and kissed him feverishly. Lucien let out a soft low, noise, almost like a purr. Tyler's blood soared.

"Good evening to you, too," Lucien murmured into the kiss.

Tyler could only growl and grind himself against Lucien's hip.

"Humans," he chuckled against Tyler's hair as Tyler moved his mouth to his neck. "You're so hot, so fast. I wish... Ah—" Lucien cut off when Tyler found a way to get his hand under his clothing and brushed his fingers over one of his nipples.

"I bet I can get you hot, Lucien," Tyler panted against his skin.

"Tyler," he started but Tyler claimed his mouth again and threw his leg over Lucien's. Tyler felt the haemophile shiver, and his own arousal flamed.

"You wanted me to tell you how I was feeling," Tyler said in a rush. "Hearing how turned on I was turned you on." Lucien just breathed heavily into the dark as Tyler ran his lips up his jaw to nip his earlobe, continuing to work his nipple and thrusting his erection against Lucien's side. "I'm what you need. I know it."

Lucien slid his arms around Tyler and rolled them so Lucien was on top. His delicious weight made Tyler shudder with pleasure. He ran his hands over his clothed back, his ass, his thighs, drinking in the long, slow kiss.

Just when Tyler was starting to get desperate, Lucien broke the kiss. Tension wafted through the darkness between them like smoke.

"What is it?"

Lucien's weight shifted across his hips, and he opened the cell. Light flooded in. Tyler blinked until his eyes adjusted. His chest filled with ice water when he took in the hard, distant look on Lucien's face.

"I can't do this again, Tyler."

"What?" Tyler propped himself on his elbows, his pulse fluttering in his throat. "What do you mean?" Lucien shifted off Tyler's body and sat against the side of the cell, gazing into nothingness. "Lucien?"

"I can't do this with a human."

Emotion spiked sharp in Tyler's chest. "Bullshit. What was all that at the compound? You saying that was nothing?"

"Of course it's not nothing," Lucien said, not meeting his eyes. "That's why it has to stop here."

"You're not making any sense."

Lucien finally looked at him. His eyes were blank as red stone. "I brought you here to keep you safe, not feed this thing between us."

"You said you wanted me. You said you wanted to help me enjoy being touched again." Tyler didn't like the audible need in his voice but couldn't keep quiet, either.

Lucien's face was so closed off that Tyler suddenly felt a fear of a very different sort.

"Have I not done that already?" he said quietly.

"It wasn't just about that," he forced out, desperate for it to be true. "There's more here. *You* want more. I can feel it."

Lucien's eyes flickered. "I've enjoyed what we've done. But now it has to end. I can't do this with a human."

"Why not?"

"Humans change, Tyler," he said softly. "Or die."

Tyler searched for words but hurt and anger choked his throat. He sat up, fighting the urge to reach out. "Now who's scared, huh?"

"I am scared. Whatever this is between us, it's…potent." Lucien drew a shaking breath and finally something showed in his eyes — something heated and barely controlled. Desire rekindled in Tyler's chest. His throat ached. "It's too dangerous."

"I'm. Not. Scared."

Lucien put his hand on Tyler's face. The skin was cool, the long fingernails the tiniest flare of sharpness in the comfort of the touch.

"There's a life out there waiting for you. You've already wasted enough of it on me."

"I'm not even close to done with you," Tyler growled. He took Lucien's face in his hands and brought his mouth to his. Lucien went stiff as stone for a moment but then opened his mouth with a moan that was almost pained, and Tyler was possessing his mouth. Desire spiked through Tyler's flesh and took control. He grabbed Lucien's arms and pulled him into the padding, crushing his body to him and tilting his head to deepen the kiss. Lucien's hair fell like a fragrant curtain around them, and his lithe body warmed to Tyler's touch.

"Tyler," he whispered between panting breaths, "we can do this, if that's what you want. But…"

"No buts," Tyler ordered, digging his fingers into Lucien's arse and thrusting his groin against him. "We're not thinking right now. We're just feeling. I want to make you feel something again. I want to make you come. I need to see it. Feel it."

Lucien sighed and melted into Tyler's embrace. Tyler had never known a desire so strong. He wanted to rip Lucien's clothes off and plunge straight into him, make him forget everything but him, see if he could make him scream with pleasure. But from the distant remoteness that still hung around Lucien like a curtain, he knew his usual roughness would do nothing but get himself off...and fast.

He bit his lip to damp the fire in his chest and slowly pulled at the hem of Lucien's jumper. Lucien lifted his arms and allowed it to be drawn off over his head. Then Tyler sat up and started on the buttons of his shirt. He did them one by one, slowly, leaning in and nuzzling the angle between Lucien's jaw and his neck. Tyler didn't think he'd ever be able to get enough of Lucien's skin. The delicate, wild scent of him went straight to Tyler's groin.

"Why, Tyler?" Lucien whispered as he tilted his head so Tyler could reach more of his neck with his lips.

Lucien inhaled sharply as Tyler pushed his shirt off his shoulders and ran his tongue to his collarbone. "You know why."

"I don't." Lucien let out a low moan when Tyler bent farther and licked his nipple. He wove his long fingers into Tyler's hair, and he was gratified to feel Lucien's legs tighten across his thighs.

Tyler lifted his head to look directly into Lucien's impossible eyes. "You're crazy. You're gorgeous. You're bloody terrifying, and I've wanted you more than I've ever wanted anything."

"You really were never scared of me," Lucien whispered, his eyes darkening. "You wanted this — and you were scared to admit it."

Tyler kissed him again, thrusting his tongue deep into his mouth to taste the smokiness of him. He ran his hands up Lucien's toned back, loving the coolness, the firmness, the strength he felt there.

He wrapped his arms around Lucien and maneuvered them so he was on his back then unfastened his trousers. Lucien continued to kiss him, making low, intimate noises and running his fingers through Tyler's hair and down his neck. Tyler pushed his trousers down and lifted himself just long enough to rid himself of his shirt, then bent again to lick and mouth Lucien's neck and chest.

Lucien's breathing finally began to quicken. His eyes were closed, and his mouth was open. He was achingly beautiful with his head back and his body arching to meet Tyler's ministrations. Tyler grasped his cock and was gratified to find it starting to swell.

"Tyler," Lucien gasped as he began to work the stiffening flesh. Tyler fluttered kisses over his belly and the top of his toned thighs.

"I want you completely naked, Lucien," he said against the soft skin of his hip. "I want to see all of you."

"You'll have to stand up then," Lucien murmured, and a thrill went up Tyler's spine to hear the mingled desire and amusement in his tone.

Tyler sat on his heels and fumbled at his jeans while Lucien stripped off the rest of his clothing. Tyler threw all their clothes out of the cell and claimed his mouth again, running his hands over all the exposed flesh.

"That strip you did was so hot," Tyler mumbled. "Teasing me like that. You knew just what you were doing."

Lucien smiled against Tyler's mouth and dragged his fingernails down Tyler's back. "You were fired by your imagination then," he whispered. "How is reality comparing?"

Tyler only moaned and eased him back into the soft lining cell, pushing his knees apart to lie between them. He kissed him deep and thrust against the hot space between his legs. He fought back the red wave of orgasm threatening to sweep him away and concentrated on Lucien's skin. He moved from his jaw to his neck to his chest, lapping at each nipple in turn. Lucien's breath hitched in his throat, and he lifted his hips. Tyler's nerves sang to feel the firm flesh of his growing erection pressing on his chest.

He moved farther down and took the long, half-hard cock into his mouth. Lucien gasped. Tyler shuddered to taste the heady flavor of the tender skin and lapped at him greedily. Lucien moaned and his thighs tensed under Tyler's hands. Tyler worked him with his mouth, feeling him swell against his tongue. He slid his hands around Lucien's knees, slowly lifting them and pushing them apart.

Lucien was silent now, though he was panting heavily, his head back, lips parted, eyes shut. Tyler lifted his head from Lucien's cock long enough to liberally coat two of his fingers with saliva. Lucien's eyes fluttered open, and his gaze locked on Tyler's.

"Do you want it this way?" Tyler said, voice low and hard, praying for him to say yes.

"Yes, Tyler," Lucien breathed. "I want it this way. Want *you* this way."

Tyler's breath swelled in his chest, and he eased his fingers into Lucien's tight entrance, not breaking eye contact.

Lucien inhaled, deep and slow. Tyler reached deeper. Lucien threw his head back and opened his mouth in a silent scream. Tyler grinned before lowering his head to once again suck on Lucien's cock as he worked his entrance with two, then three fingers.

His own need was a knot in his belly. When he'd done this with Damon, he'd come in under a minute. He had to pace himself. Lucien had his fists clenched as his sides, and his cock jerked in Tyler's mouth. Tyler burned with pleasure as color flushed into his face, but also chafed to be buried into the delicious space he was exploring with his fingers.

He adjusted his angle, swept them deep and around and, finally, Lucien cried out.

"Tyler," he called. "Tyler, *now*."

Tyler moaned, crawled up, plunged his tongue into his mouth and guided the end of his cock into Lucien's body. He gasped into Tyler's mouth as he slid in all in one go. Tyler forgot to breathe. He was dizzy with the feel of it. He told himself to hold back, hold still, go slow…but he couldn't.

He propped himself on one elbow, lifted one of Lucien's legs with his free hand to deepen his thrust, pulled out and plunged in again. He groaned, closed his eyes and did it again, his control completely stripped away. He pounded into Lucien, his own cries hoarse in his ears — the smell, feel and sound of Lucien's responses surrounding and drowning him.

Lightning coursed through his body, scouring his nerve endings to ash. But still, he couldn't stop. He was dimly aware of Lucien's fingernails digging into his back and the distant sound of his cries, but the roaring in his ears drowned out everything but the overwhelming pleasure.

It may have been five seconds or five hours later before Tyler felt an orgasm like a tornado swirling behind his balls. He fumbled blindly for Lucien's cock, his hand slippery with sweat. He pumped it as he came so hard his awareness spiraled away like dust in the storm wind.

When his vision returned, he was breathing like he'd run a marathon. He was slumped on Lucien's chest, still buried deep inside him. His cock was still throbbing. Lucien's breathing was calm and slow. Tyler registered this with a jerk of panic then became aware of the warm stickiness between their bellies.

He lifted himself on trembling limbs and gazed into Lucien's face. The color had already left it, but his eyes were flaming rubies, as bright as sunrise, saturated with sated desire.

"Was that—?"

Lucien cut him off with a deep, long kiss. "It was wonderful," he whispered.

# Chapter Seven

They lay twined in each other's limbs for a long time after. Tyler's breathing slowed and the sweat dried on his skin. He shivered but still didn't want to move away. He still couldn't entirely explain to himself what he was feeling.

It should be over. The itch should be scratched.

But he wanted to do it all over again...and *now*. He raised his head as his cock pulsed against Lucien's leg.

Lucien was unsmiling. "Tyler...I can't."

Tyler lowered his head back to the soft pillow. He trailed his fingers lazily over Lucien's skin, ignoring the uncertainty prickling up his spine.

"So what happens now?"

"I should feed," Lucien said in a low voice, "and rest. Wait for the last of that drug to leave my system." He raised his eyes. "You should stay here with me, until my strength returns. I don't think it's safe for you to leave until it does."

Tyler grunted and rested his head back against his arm. "I'm not afraid of Damon."

Lucien closed his eyes. "So rash, Tyler. So reckless."

"If I weren't, I never would have met you."

"True."

"So we lay low here for a bit. Then what?" Lucien didn't answer. The look on his face made a knot form in Tyler's stomach. Silence bloomed between them. Tyler shifted with the need to say something. He opened his mouth but all that came out was, "How will you, you know...eat?"

"There will be flasks in the fridge. Though, nothing for you, I'm afraid."

"I'll be fine," he said, propping his head up on his hand. Lucien gazed up at him, a ghost of curiosity in his eyes.

"So, now we've done it twice... Will you, you know...tell me more?"

Lucien frowned, confusion clouding his eyes. "Tell you what?"

"I dunno." Tyler shrugged. "Where you're from? Your real name? Something about your family? Anything."

Lucien closed his eyes for a moment. When he opened them again they were remote and distant. "I don't remember any of those things."

Tyler stared at him. "What?"

Lucien sighed and extricated himself from Tyler's legs and climbed out of the cell. "Those things belong to my human life. That has been dead and buried for centuries."

Tyler sat up, frowning. "You don't remember anything?"

He shook his head. "That's not who I am anymore."

"I don't get it," Tyler said, rubbing his head. "How can your real name and where you come from not matter to you?"

"It's not a case of mattering. It just no longer exists," Lucien said, dressing without looking at him. "I am who my maker made me."

Tyler blinked. "Your maker?"

Lucien buttoned his shirt slowly. "The one that turned me, made me like her."

"Her?" Lucien looked at him. Tyler fidgeted and looked away. "Okay, so *she* must know who you were and where you came from?"

"She may have," Lucien said, pulling on his jumper. He moved to a small fridge under a counter and opened it. "I don't remember her ever telling me. And I didn't ask. It wasn't important."

"*How* is it not important?" Tyler said, climbing out of the cell and pulling on his underwear. His skin felt raw with the uncertainty that simmered under it, making irritation bloom to disguise the deeper, scarier feelings underneath.

Lucien shrugged as he took a silver flask from the fridge and unscrewed it. The metallic smell made Tyler wince. He looked away as Lucien drank.

"That life is gone," he said quietly. "She gave me a new one."

Tyler raised his head. Lucien's gaze was far away. There was something unfamiliar about the set of his face Tyler didn't exactly like.

"Who is she? The one that made you?"

"I knew her as Ioana, though that was probably one of many names she had over the years."

"Knew?"

Lucien drank again. "She's been dead for a long time. A very, very long time."

Tyler pulled on his shirt, unsure what to say. "Shit. Sorry."

Lucien's smile was thin. "I don't think you are."

Tyler looked away. "What *do* you remember, then?"

Lucien gazed at the wall. "I remember back to the time I was turned."

"When was that?"

"I don't know the year, not exactly. But I know it was somewhere in the sixteenth century."

Tyler's mouth fell open. "That's...wow."

"Getting on for six centuries now." Lucien gave him a strange smile. "It sounds like a long time, but time doesn't mean the same thing when you have that much of it."

"How does that work?"

"You measure things in different ways—important events, people in your life, changes in the world." He stared at the floor. "I've seen so many of those I can't keep up with them anymore."

Tyler pulled on his T-shirt and leaned against the sleeping cell. "That's why you wanted Damon to...?"

Lucien was quiet a long moment. "I've tried existing apart from the world. And I've tried changing." He raised his eyes. "Nothing worked."

"Life throws stuff at you all the time," Tyler responded quietly. "You don't walk away from something just 'cause it's hard."

The corner of a smile lifted Lucien's mouth. He came close and looked down at him. "You're very special. I hope you know that."

"I've been called all sorts of things over the years...never special."

Lucien brushed his fingers over Tyler's hair with a thoughtful expression. "Well, you are."

Tyler couldn't tear his eyes away from Lucien's face. "What was the world like? All the way back then?"

Lucien's gaze went far away. "It was a much larger place, with a lot fewer people in it." He frowned. "All the languages were different. Nature was different…"

"Climate change and that?"

Lucien put his head on one side. "Partly. But also because there were still places that no human had ever been to before. Places that no one owned. The world still belonged to itself." He drew a deep breath. "There was this place in the mountains where Ioana and I would go. It was so quiet, so peaceful—just the trees, the rocks, the snow and the sky." His mouth was soft, his expression thoughtful. "There are human settlements closer now, of course. But I went back, once, not so long ago. Our place was still there. Still secret."

"What sort of place?"

He met Tyler's gaze and smiled. "I supposed you'd call it a castle. It's built into a cliff, surrounded by trees and rock faces. No human could reach it. Even Ioana didn't know who'd built it, only that it had sheltered our kind for centuries. There are caves to sleep in and wide, wide windows overlooking the mountains and the sky. The snow in the winter was so perfect it was like it had been painted. And in the summer, when the plants and the animals filled the air with scents and song…" He breathed deeply and sighed it out. "I wished more than once that it could be my whole life."

"No people? No phones? No internet?"

"Nothing but the house, the mountain and the weather." Lucien's voice had changed. It was softer, more human.

"That sounds…"—he fought for a word then heard himself say—"quiet."

Lucien's expression turned thoughtful. "I think you'd like it."

Tyler looked away. "Must be so weird — remembering what people were like back then and knowing what we are like now."

"Humans were still human, then. Evil was as prevalent as it is now." He gave a sad smile. "Some things don't change."

"Surely it was worse back then," Tyler insisted. "Beheadings and hangings and wars and all the stuff like that."

"That all still happens now, my dear," Lucien said, running a finger down Tyler's face. "More than it ever did — because there are more humans."

Tyler shook his head. "We can't be all that bad."

"Oh, far from it," Lucien said, taking Tyler's face in his hands and tilting it to gaze into his eyes. "You are beautiful creatures. Fragile. Passionate. Each one so full of potential. Why do you think my kind risked coming out of the shadows to live among you?"

Tyler whispered, "What's it like, Lucien? What's it really like?"

"What?"

"Being like you."

Lucien dropped his hands. He moved to a chair and sat, turning the flask around in his hands.

"I've been very lucky in a lot of ways," Lucien eventually said, "having the life I've had. I've seen extraordinary things, met extraordinary people, witnessed time shape the world around me. But through it all, I'm a constant...unchanging." He frowned slightly. "My purpose has never changed. That's the problem."

"What purpose?"

Lucien examined him. "You know what purpose, Tyler."

Tyler frowned harder. "I do?"

"The list?" Lucien said quietly. "Those people? *They* are the reason Ioana brought me over. The reason haemophiles, as you call us, exist at all."

Tyler shook his head. "I don't understand."

"We exist to watch over humankind. To guard it from the worst of itself."

"You're having me on," Tyler said, though the look on Lucien's face drained his certainty.

"I assure you I'm not." Lucien leaned forward with his elbows on his knees, his eyes intent. "My maker called it the Gift of the Blood. We have been gifted the power of God, to watch over and protect His children...a serious and solemn purpose." He looked at the floor. "And that's what I've done — or tried to do, all these years."

"You believe..." Tyler fumbled, "you believe you're God?"

Lucien narrowed his eyes. "Not God. A vessel for his powers, only."

Tyler shook his head. "You can't seriously believe that."

"That's what I was taught."

Tyler struggled not to break eye contact. "And God wants you to kill people for him?"

"Yes."

Tyler clamped his mouth shut. He dropped his gaze.

"You don't believe me."

"I get religion was a big deal in the sixteenth century," Tyler said carefully. "But it's not the same thing anymore."

"There still has to be a reason we do what we do."

"Why?"

Lucien frowned. "What?"

"Why does there have to be a reason? Can't we just be hurtling through the universe in chaos?"

Lucien raised his eyebrows.

"So," Tyler fumbled, "everyone on that list? Every last name? They really were all, what? Evil?"

"That's right."

Tyler winced. "And you get to decide what's evil, do you?"

"Of course not," Lucien said simply. "Morality decides that. Human values that build the very foundation of who you are. Ones that have remained undisputed for millennia."

Tyler raised his eyebrows. "I find it hard to believe there is any moral that hasn't been disputed at some point in history."

Lucien waved a hand. "You're overcomplicating it. This is about your gut…your instinct. Right and wrong. You've made the same judgments yourself. Many times."

"I don't *kill* people, Lucien," Tyler said, exasperatedly.

"Maybe you would, if you could."

Tyler made an impatient noise and looked away. "Fine, answer me this. Have you ever…got it wrong?"

"Got what wrong?"

"Have you ever killed the wrong person? An innocent person?"

"No."

"Never?"

"Never."

Tyler lifted his gaze to the ceiling. "This is so crazy."

"It's not. It's simple. The Blood protects us from sickness, from aging. It gives us strength. But it's not for nothing. It carries a great responsibility."

"So you believe God made haemophiles to be some sort of vigilante death squad?"

Lucien's face was blank. "It's not a joke."

"I'm not laughing," Tyler said, sitting on the edge of the sofa. "Lucien, this is insane."

"So you're apparently telling yourself. But you see things the same way."

Tyler opened and closed his mouth a few times, shook his head and let out a humorless laugh. "Making sure a scumbag doesn't get away with rape is not the same thing as believing you were put on the planet on some sort of holy quest to *kill* people."

"I never said it was holy," Lucien cut in. "Ioana used that word. I never did. But we serve a higher truth—something beyond us, bigger than us...a greater good."

Tyler stared at him. "You really believe this, don't you?"

"Why else would we exist?" Lucien spread his hands. "What other possible explanation could there be? We didn't evolve like other creatures. We don't breed. We don't die. What is our purpose, apart from to be the shadow of humanity? Its dark side? The eyes, ears and thirst that balances its good and its evil?"

Tyler shook his head. "How come no one else has ever mentioned this? In all the press statements, all the blogs, all the research, not a single other haemo has said anything about anything like this."

Anger sharpened Lucien's face. "Ioana is gone. As are all the others that remembered this. *Believed* this. I am the last one." His troubled gaze shifted to the wall. "Emory warned me. And he was right. I am redundant—or, worse, have become a force for destruction."

"Emory...that's the baron, right?"

"That's right."

Tyler swallowed. "He was the one that stopped you from killing me."

"He did. He is more adjusted to this world. He always thought he could help me adjust, too. A foolish hope."

Tyler swallowed. "How do you know each other?"

"I brought him over."

Tyler started. "You made him? Into a haemophile?"

"Yes."

"Why?"

Lucien brushed the chair arm, a slight frown on his face. "Ioana had been dead a long time by then. Many others like her were gone, too. My kind was losing its way. I thought it was time to do my bit—to recruit another."

Tyler swallowed. "So he agreed to do this…this work, too?"

Lucien didn't move or wave his arms. "No. He refused."

"So why turn him?"

"I thought I could convince him. And I was weary of being an army of one. I was weary…" He swallowed. "I was weary of being alone."

Silence filled the room. Tyler didn't want to ask the question, but it roared in his head like a rushing wind, demanding to be vented. "You and Emory. And you and Ioana. Were you…you know?"

"Were we what?"

"You know…together?"

"Do you mean, were we lovers?"

Tyler winced. "Sure. I guess."

Lucien surprised Tyler with a low laugh. "I forget how prescriptive you need reality to be. Emory and I? Yes, I suppose you could say we were. We had a physical relationship, if that's what you mean. But it was more than that, much more—as it was with Ioana."

An ugly swirl of jealousy fogged through Tyler's chest at the look on Lucien's face. "More?"

"We have this bond with our makers—something more than love, more than family." Lucien met Tyler's eyes, and the look in them was dark and unfamiliar. "Something unbreakable."

"So, this bond..." Tyler fumbled, pulling at a loose thread in the sofa fabric. "You still have that with that Emory guy?"

Lucien drained the flask and put it aside. His skin had colored, and there was a spark in his eyes. "Yes. I do."

Tyler stared at the wall, unhappiness swelling in him like a balloon. He jumped to find Lucien standing in front of him. He lowered himself to his knees and put his hands on Tyler's thighs. He gazed into his face.

"The Maker and the Turned are linked by the Blood. There is nothing else like that bond in existence." His eyes were bright. Tyler couldn't understand what to make of the look in them. "But I still lost them, Tyler," he whispered. "Ioana died. Emory left me. And now he has a daughter. And a human as his life partner."

Tyler drew a shuddering breath. "Truelove."

Lucien's mouth twitched. "An appropriately named young man, perhaps."

"What are you saying here, Lucien?'

Lucien raised himself and brushed his lips over Tyler's. "I'm saying all relationships are complicated. There are no answers, no rules." He kissed him deep, then pulled away. His breathing was heavy. His eyes were bright with what Tyler thought may have been fear. It made his heart skip about. "And I can't do it again. I can't do any of it anymore."

"Not this again."

"I'm trying to explain—"

"I don't want to hear it."

"Tyler," Lucien said gently, sitting back on the edge of the chair. "Can't you see, now, why I should have stayed behind?"

"No," Tyler said firmly. "I don't."

"When I leave here, I will be hunted—hated, lost, alone, adrift without purpose. Again."

"There has to be another way."

"I've tried to find one...for years. Don't you think I've tried?"

Tyler's chest was aching, but he made himself say the words. "You could go home..."

Lucien frowned. "I don't have a home."

"That place...in the mountains. That sure sounded like you were talking about a home." Lucien went very still. "Yeah," Tyler continued, a little shakily, but whether it was with nerves or excitement he couldn't tell. "Go back to your castle place. No one will find you. You'd be safe there."

Lucien looked at the wall.

"It sounded like you liked it."

"I do."

"And you said it was all out on its own, far away from anyone. Humans can't get to it."

Lucien looked down at his hands. "I have done that in the past. Retreated there when it all got too much."

"So?"

Lucien's mouth twitched. "Running away doesn't change anything."

"You can learn to live for yourself," Tyler said, standing. "Forget about this stupid mission."

Lucien gave a half-smile. "Leave behind my reason for being?"

"It's *not* your reason for being," Tyler insisted, walking over to him and sitting on the arm of his chair. "That can be whatever you want it to be."

"You can't change your nature just because you want to."

"'Course you can," Tyler scoffed. "You just have to, you know…adjust your priorities."

Lucien was smiling, but the ruby depths of his eyes were swimming with uncertainty. "I think I can see why so many of us choose to connect with humans these days."

"You see things differently when you don't live forever."

Lucien took Tyler's hand. He ran his fingertips over the back of it, making Tyler's skin prickle and the hairs stand up on his skin.

"So?"

Lucien's eyebrows twitched. "You think I should leave. Run away. Hide?"

Tyler's chest tightened. "If it's that or letting Damon or the police get their hands on you…yes. Why not?"

Lucien looked up at him. "You've never run away from anything in your life."

"I ran away from you," he said quietly.

"And look how that turned out."

They stared hard at each other. Then Tyler leaned in and kissed him. Lucien sighed into the kiss and ran his long fingers around Tyler's neck, pulling him closer, tilting his head to sweep his tongue into Tyler's mouth.

Soon they were shuddering and panting and pawing at each other's clothing again. Tyler stripped Lucien to the skin hurriedly but then slowed his pace, kneeling between his knees where he sat on the chair and worshipped every inch of his skin with lips, tongue and hands, gratified to find him soon growing hard and gripping the arms of the chair.

Tyler stroked himself slowly as he ran his tongue over Lucien's nipples, his belly, his shoulders. Then he lifted his head, locked gazes with Lucien and began sucking his own fingers, one after the other.

Lucien watched him with parted lips, his breathing heavy, his eyes burning like the embers of a rekindled fire.

"How have you done this to me, Tyler?" he said in a breathy voice. "How do you do this and change everything?"

Tyler didn't answer. He didn't need to. When they were both hard, Lucien drew him to his feet and sat forward to lick and suck his erection. Tyler moaned, his knees quivering, sliding his fingers into Lucien's silken hair.

When he thought he was about to burst, Lucien stood and nipped at his earlobe.

"Again, Tyler," he whispered hoarsely into Tyler's ear. "I want you to do it to me again. Make me forget. Bring me into the now."

Tyler growled and backed Lucien toward the sleeping cell, running his hands down Lucien's back and cupping his arse while ravishing his mouth. His cock trembled, wet with Lucien's saliva.

Lucien bumped into the cell but instead of climbing in he turned, grasped the edge and bent over.

Tyler fought for control, hastily sucked his fingers and slid two inside. Lucien's grip tightened on the edge of the cell. He made a wordless noise and pushed back onto Tyler's fingers. Tyler worked him harder, sweeping and spreading, but he could only manage a few seconds before he was aching too much to be inside him. He withdrew his fingers and eased the end of his cock in.

Lucien shivered and threw his head back, his hair sliding against his spine and shoulders.

Tyler grasped his hips, savoring the anticipation, then slid slowly in.

The fire was even hotter than last time. The itch was nowhere near scratched. He made himself stick to a slow, steady rhythm, closing his eyes, holding tight, concentrating on the sensation of pushing in and pulling out of Lucien, over and over, not quite able to believe how he was feeling, not quite able to trust the intensity of it.

Lucien panted heavily, thrusting against Tyler as he moved, meeting him and swaying with him in a beat as natural as breathing.

He slid his arms around Lucien's chest, absorbing the feeling of him, inside and out, never ceasing his penetration, unable to admit there could be an end to this.

But the fire was building. The sparks were gathering—lazily this time, like fireflies waking at the start of night. But more and more blinked and glittered into existence, growing brighter. His breathing was labored, his limbs were trembling.

"Lucien," he growled into his ear as he thrust in, over and over. "Lucien, I'm gonna come."

Lucien sighed, gripped Tyler's hand and guided it toward his quivering cock. "Me, too."

Tyler pumped him, once, twice, three times.

Lucien cried out and went limp in his arms. His body bunched around Tyler's cock and the world dissolved into waves of blinding ecstasy.

Lucien was kissing him. He was kissing him, running his hands over him, muttering and mumbling nonsensical words.

"Wha...what?" Tyler muttered dumbly, brain fuzzy, his skin hypersensitive to the touch.

"Again, Tyler," Lucien whispered, nuzzling his jaw and his neck. "Again."

Tyler let out a shaky laugh. "You want to do it again?"

"And again," Lucien said, grasping his softening cock, making him gasp. "All night long. Don't let it end."

Tyler grinned against Lucien's shoulder, held him close and kissed his skin. "I can do that."

# Chapter Eight

When Tyler next woke, he was groggy and sore in all the best ways. He blinked in the low light and finally registered that he was sprawled on the silk lining of the sleeping cell. He was naked and sticky. Everything smelled like sex…and Lucien. The tremble of returning desire began to prickle along his nerves, but his mouth was dry, his head was aching.

He sat up with a groan.

Lucien stood by the fridge, draining a flask. He looked fresh and rested, his cool skin glowing, his red eyes burning with a low light. He smiled.

"Good evening…again."

Tyler blinked and stared around at the blank walls. "We slept through another day?"

"We did," Lucien said. "We were worn out."

"I'll say," Tyler said, wincing as he climbed out of the cell on wobbly legs. "Don't think I've fucked that hard in my life."

"I'm flattered."

Lucien's smile was doing all sorts of confusing things to Tyler. But he found it hard to focus as he reached for his scattered clothing.

"Not much longer," Lucien said, coming forward to help. "We're leaving tonight."

Tyler blinked. "We are?"

Lucien nodded. "My strength is back. I'll help you get somewhere you can charge your phone and call for help."

Tyler went still. "Then what?"

Lucien's expression was guarded. "Then you go home."

"And what about you?"

Lucien didn't answer.

"Lucien," Tyler started but Lucien pressed a finger to his lips.

"You're thirsty and hungry, Tyler," he insisted. "We need to get you home. That's all that matters right now."

"But—"

Lucien stiffened. His eyes were dark and blank. He held Tyler utterly still. When Tyler tried to move, he just held him tighter.

"They're coming."

"Who?" Tyler said. Lucien loosened his hold. Tyler blinked. Lucien was gone.

A cold draft rushed through the room. Tyler hurried to the stairs. The door at the top stood open. Tyler raced up, adrenaline needling in his veins.

"Lucien?" he called, stepping out into the darkness. He could just make out the pale outline of the outside door. He opened his mouth to call again when an iron-hard grip fastened on his wrist then he was being dragged out the door.

"You have to run, Tyler," Lucien said. "Run harder than you've ever run. You won't outrun them, but once they have me they won't—"

"Wait. Stop." Tyler dug his heels into the leafy ground, dragging against Lucien's grip but he was too strong.

"You have to go," Lucien insisted, desperation tightening his tone. In the moonlight his face was a hard mask, his glowing eyes wide and urgent. "Now."

"Who's coming? Damon?"

"Not Damon."

"Then who."

Lucien bared his teeth. "Emory."

Tyler blinked. "What will he do?"

"It doesn't matter."

Tyler planted his feet. "I'm not leaving you."

"Tyler."

"No, whatever this is, we face it together."

Lucien's face twisted, his teeth bared and glinting in the moonlight. "They'll use you against me. They'll—"

"Lucien... Good of you to wait for us."

Out of the shadows stepped a ring of haemophiles, at least half a dozen. Tyler staggered and would have fallen but for Lucien's grip on him. The moonlight glinted in their eyes like cats-eye reflectors. They enclosed Lucien and Tyler, blocking every escape.

"You know why we're here, don't you?" The one that had spoken must have been well over six feet high. His hair was as red as rust, and Tyler could make out an exquisite suit, patent leather shoes, flashing emerald eyes. Behind him stood the looming form of Baron Emory Von Magnusson. The others stuck to the shadows, power and strength evident in every line of their bodies.

"I do not answer to you, Darragh Kelly," Lucien said in a low, dangerous voice. "Or to any of you."

"Let the human go, Lucien," Magnusson said, his voice surging like a sea storm. "Don't make me make you."

"I can speak for myself, you know," Tyler said, shrugging himself out of Lucien's grip and stepping between him and the haemophiles. "And just what the hell do you all want with him, anyway?"

"Tyler," Lucien warned.

"Mr. Lomax, as I live and breathe." The red-haired haemophile's eyes landed on Tyler like lead weights. The hint of the Irish accent rippled in his words like whiskey. "Every time there's trouble, we seem to find you."

"Darragh," Magnusson started, stepping to his side, but Kelly lifted a hand.

"This situation is delicate enough, Emory," he said firmly. "And you are too close to it. Lucien. We told you what would happen if you crossed the line again."

"There is no line," Lucien said. The tone of his voice catapulted Tyler back to that freezing winter night on Askham Moor. The unmistakable threat was like a gunshot in the air.

"We warned you," Kelly repeated, apparently unperturbed. "Now the human police are after you. Your mess is all over the papers. It will be months before we know the true extent of the damage. Years before we can undo it — if we ever can."

"And what about the damage the world is doing to itself?" Lucien said, his eyes blazing in the darkness. "The untold disasters playing out as we very speak, unchecked, while you all stand here accusing me —"

"You're a dinosaur, Lucien," said one of the other haemophiles, his words sharp as glass. "A medieval anachronism. And we've let you roam wild and unchecked long enough."

"You are all frightened children," Lucien replied, eyes flashing. "You don't understand."

"Lucien," Tyler pleaded. "Tell them you're not going to hurt anyone anymore. Tell them—" Tyler swore when someone grabbed his arm in a grip like iron and dragged him to the side. The more he struggled, the harder the grip became, bruising his bones and breaking his skin. He swallowed a cry of pain.

"Let him go," Lucien demanded.

"You've never allowed a human this close to you that you weren't planning to kill or turn, Lucien." Magnusson said. He was well over a foot taller than Lucien, but Lucien didn't lift his head to meet the penetrating gaze, instead glaring from under his eyelashes with a face as fearful as a demon from a nightmare. "This is for his safety…and yours."

"You never understood, Emory," Lucien breathed. "*Never.*"

Magnusson shook his head. "No. I didn't."

"Emory," Kelly said, stepping forward. "We had an agreement."

Magnusson took a shaking breath. "You have to come with us now, Lucien, so we can fix this."

"How?" Tyler demanded. "How are you going to fix it? Kill him and bury his body somewhere it will never be found? How does that make you any better than him?"

"Stay out of this, Mr. Lomax," Kelly said wearily, nodding to the other haemophiles, who began to close in.

"You're worse than hypocrites. At least he only kills people who deserve it."

"Mr. Lomax," Kelly said, his voice harder than iron. "I don't expect the likes of you to understand, but I'm shedding blood, sweat and tears so our kind can be thought of as people — people who care, hurt, love." Something had changed about the haemophile's voice and face. Uncertainty ghosted through Tyler. He glanced at Lucien, whose eyes were still locked on the unflinching baron. "Lucien can't be part of this model. He's proved it time and time again. It's too late. He'll ruin everything."

"You don't know that," Tyler protested.

"If I thought you could do what was needed, Emory," Lucien cut in, his mouth barely moving, "I would go willingly. But you lack the courage it takes to have such a conviction."

"We can find a way, Lucien," Magnusson said. "We've found ways before."

"Exile?" Lucien scowled, baring his teeth. "It doesn't work."

"You *said*," Tyler pleaded. "You said you would escape, Lucien. You said you would go away…for me. *Tell* them."

Magnusson looked at him. Pain glinted in the dark blue of his eyes. He opened his mouth to say something but then there was a rushing noise, and Lucien had vanished. The haemophiles muttered and gasped, casting around. The one holding Tyler muttered in another language and started pulling him away. There came a violent jerk, and Tyler was freed. He staggered forward.

Arms closed around him, and he was lifted bodily from the ground. The shouts and protests of the confused haemophiles died away. Tyler felt like he was flying, moving too fast to see, to hear, to understand anything.

The wind smelled of leaves, of grass, farmyards, car exhaust. They moved in and out of streetlights, too fast for Tyler to even sense a direction, let alone make out where they were going.

Eventually, Lucien slowed to the point where Tyler could tell he was running, leaping walls and fences, dodging around trees before Tyler had even seen they were in the path. Then, finally, he slowed further and stopped altogether. He set Tyler on the ground. He staggered. Lucien caught him. Tyler reached out in the dark, found a drystone wall and slowly collapsed onto it, hung his head between his knees and wretched.

He hadn't eaten in almost two days, so hardly anything came up. Lucien rubbed his back gently until the sickness faded. He straightened, wiping his mouth on his shirt, breathing in the cool night air until his head stopped spinning.

"Sorry," Lucien said. "I had to get you away from them. They wouldn't have hurt you," he added at the look on Tyler's face. "But they would have handed you over to the authorities. They wouldn't have hurt me, either, just so you know. Whatever impression they gave you, that was never their intention."

"Then what were they going to do?"

Lucien shrugged. "Given me the standard lecture — like I haven't heard it thousands of times over hundreds of years. Then escorted me to the edge of civilization. Turned me loose somewhere without people — out of sight, out of mind. It's a dance we've danced before. They know it doesn't work. Eventually, I get drawn back — or humans get drawn to me. They feel they have to do it, anyway." Lucien looked over his shoulder. "We're not all that different. I'm just less willing to play their game than I was."

Tyler blinked stupidly into the dark. He groped for Lucien's hand, found it and clung on. "Will they come after you again?"

"They will try," Lucien said. "But they can't catch me. They're all too young...too slow."

"But the plan," Tyler fumbled again. "The mountains. Your castle. You said that *would* work?"

Lucien was quiet for a long time, then he stood. "I promised I'd take you somewhere safe. That's all I promised. Let me do that. Please."

Tyler's heart dipped. "I don't want to go before this is sorted."

"This is not your fight."

"Isn't that up to me?"

Lucien put his hand on Tyler's face. "You've done enough."

Tyler's heart thudded in his chest. His blood pounded in his temples. A thousand things to say, to make Lucien listen, tangled in his throat, but none came out. Lucien kissed him, a gentle, chaste touch of lips, and all the anger drained out of him. He slumped against him and allowed Lucien to draw him to his feet.

Lucien led the way, moving at human pace this time, keeping a tight grip on Tyler's hand. Clouds obscured the moon.

Lucien took them over fields, along farm tracks, over boggy moorland. Tyler's hunger had become a hard knot in his insides. He was tired and aching but didn't want to ask how much longer it would be—didn't want to think about what would happen when they got to wherever they were going.

Finally, they crested a hill and saw lights ahead. Streetlight shone on rooftops and winding streets. A car went past on the road and illuminated a road sign just visible over the hedge.

*Welcome to Illington. Please Drive Carefully.*

"Jesus," Tyler muttered as Lucien went to the gate onto the road. "We're miles from anywhere."

"The pub's open," Lucien said softly. He stood at the roadside with his hands in the pockets of his long coat. The distant streetlight gilded his pale skin in gold. His eyes, glowing like dull embers in the dark, were distant...sad. Tyler again fought for words, but nothing came. "You can charge your phone, call for a lift. Then it might be a good idea for you to go away for a while. Give Damon a chance to move on."

"Lucien... "

"You promised, Tyler," Lucien said, giving him a level look.

"I promised that I'd leave that place," Tyler said, gesturing the way they'd come. "I never promised to leave you—not before I knew you were going to be okay."

Lucien looked back over the moor. His face was unreadable. Tyler grabbed his shoulders. "Tell me you're going back to those mountains. Tell me you're going somewhere they won't find you."

"I will," he murmured in a low voice. "I'll go back to the castle. I'll stay there as long as I can."

Tyler blanched. "What does that mean?"

Lucien blinked slowly. His eyes were darker than ever. "I need a reason to exist, Tyler," he whispered. "I used to know what that was. I don't know how to carry on without it."

"There's more to you than punishing people."

Lucien put his head on one side. A smile softened his face. "I love that you think so."

"Of course there is," he insisted. "Lucien, I…" He faltered, dropped his hands. "I don't feel stuff like this…ever. I usually know what I'm doing. Where I'm going. Know what I want. But with you?" He took a deep, shaking breath. His body threatened to tremble. He clenched his fists to stop his hands from shaking. "There's more to you," he said quietly. "That's just the truth."

"Tyler," he said wearily, "you're so young. You can't possibly understand —"

"You're so old you've forgotten it, that's all," Tyler said hurriedly. "You've lived so long by some else's rules, you can't see anything else. I'm new enough to see that things could be different."

Lucien looked away.

Tyler grabbed his hand. "What about me?" Lucien raised his eyes. Tyler made the words come out. "Can't I be your reason?"

"We hardly know each other," Lucien whispered.

"And yet you've taken over my life," Tyler said. "Night and day. Asleep and awake. You are all I've thought about. And you?" He reached out a trembling hand and threaded into the hair at the nape of Lucien's nape. "You're still here."

Lucien frowned. "Sorry?"

"Magnusson told you to leave that night on the moor. I heard him. But you didn't."

Lucien lowered his gaze.

"You found out so much about me. About where I live. Then you started hunting the evil people in my city. Why?"

Lucien let out a long sigh then rested his forehead against Tyler's. "I don't understand any of this," he whispered. "I've lived the same way for almost six hundred years. Then you changed everything in one night. How did you do that, Tyler?"

"It's okay to be scared," Tyler said, his voice tight, feeling like he was talking to himself even more than Lucien. "Change is scary."

Lucien was quiet for a long time. Finally, he raised his head. His expression was unreadable. "I'll try," he whispered. "I'll try what you suggested, Tyler. I'll try to live just for myself. By myself. In the mountains. But I won't try anything until I know you're safe."

Tyler almost wilted with relief. He clutched Lucien's shoulders tighter to stay upright. Lucien grasped him by the elbows. "Okay," he mumbled. "I'll go. I'll get out of here…if you promise to do the same thing."

Silence swam between them again. Lucien's grip tightened.

"This means saying goodbye," he whispered.

Tyler nodded. His throat closed over. He cleared it with a cough. "I know," he said. "It sucks. But life sucks. I already knew that."

Lucien swallowed. "This is going to hurt," he murmured. "Hurt both of us."

"Hurting's fine," Tyler muttered. "Hurting means you're alive."

Lucien smiled. He gathered Tyler close, rested his chin on Tyler's shoulder. Tyler wrapped his arms around Lucien and held on. Of all the dreams he'd had of being this close to Lucien, standing in a muddy field in the dark just holding him hadn't been one of them. But it meant more than anything else that had passed between them.

"Go," Lucien said, pulling away and stepping back. "It's time."

"Lucien—"

"No more, Tyler," he said, backing into the shadows. "Let this be it. Go home. Be happy."

Now the moment had come, doubt swamped Tyler. He opened his mouth to protest, to swear, to beg Lucien to take him with him, he didn't know. But he was alone.

He shuddered, despite the warmth of the night. He climbed over a gate and started plodding toward the village, feeling like he was dragging a heavy weight.

He made it to the Fox and the Hounds pub with his heart dense in his chest. Half a dozen locals sat around at small tables, chatting over their drinks. He was very aware of his disheveled, muddy clothing but no one looked up as he entered.

He bought half a lager and a cheese roll then took it all to a table in the far corner. He got his phone out of his pocket. There was a plug socket under his chair, but he didn't move to plug it in. He watched the bubbles in his drink, fizzing from the bottom to the top. Then bursting. Disappearing.

Eventually, his stomach demanded his attention. He drank the lager and swallowed half the roll. His headache eased. The dazed feeling passed. He looked around, trying to get his head around exactly how he'd ended up in the Fox and Hounds in Illington with a dead phone and an ache in his insides that had nothing to do with physical hunger.

He rubbed his face, sighed and plugged in his phone.

By the time he'd finished his food and was halfway through another drink, his phone flickered to life.

The screen was crowded with notifications. He ignored them all and dialed his sister's number.

For the first time he could actually remember, she answered on the first ring.

"Tyler." She sounded both angry and frightened. "What the hell? Where have you been?"

Tyler ran his finger through the crumbs on the table, unable to decide which part of the truth to share. "I'm in Illington."

"What? Where?"

"Illington," he repeated. "That village near Thirsk. We came here with Dad that time?"

"Christ," Emerald muttered. "That dreadful lunch with Auntie Maggie. I remember. What the hell are you doing there?"

Tyler swallowed, his mouth suddenly dry again.

"Tyler, you've been gone for days. I was this close to calling the cops."

"No," Tyler cut in. "No cops."

Emerald paused. "What have you done?"

"Nothing," he said, glancing around to make sure the other patrons were still absorbed in their beer. "I haven't…" He made an impatient noise. "Can you just come get me?"

"You got all the way out there without your car?"

"I'll explain everything, okay?" he lied. "Can you just come? I need to get out of here before…"

Tyler froze. Damon stood in the doorway. His silver eyes were as sharp as blades. His hands were in the pockets of his jacket and so was something else — something that was pointed right at Tyler.

"How did you…?"

Damon stepped to his table and spoke in a low voice. "Hang up."

Tyler gripped the phone tight.

"Tyler?" Emerald's voice was sharp. "Tyler, tell me what's going on. What—?"

"Hang. Up."

Tyler obeyed and set the phone on the table.

"Outside, I think," Damon said softly. Tyler glanced at the shape in Damon's pocket and stood. Damon nodded to the back door.

The night air had cooled, and the moon had come out. Floodlights illuminated part of a paved beer garden, but beyond that there was nothing but shadow. A stream gurgled somewhere in the dark. Damon led them out of sight of the pub's windows.

"So," he said, pulling the gun from his pocket and letting it hang by his side. "Just popped out for a pint, did you?"

"I wasn't your prisoner. At least, that's what you told me."

"You hired me to do a job," Damon said, acid in his tone, "which I intend to finish." He scanned the dark. "Where is he? Did he find somewhere to get a drink as well?"

"I'm telling you to leave it."

"Leave it?" he repeated, eyes narrow. "Leave it loose? Leave it to kill again?" Damon shook his head. "I misjudged you. I thought you were strong, but you're weak. You let him get to you."

Heat flooded Tyler's face. "He's not some rabid dog to be put down."

"That's exactly what he is," Damon said, holding the gun so tight it started to shake. "And you thought so, too—up until the point you fucked him."

"I was wrong," Tyler said. "*We* were wrong."

Damon sighed loudly and looked up at the stars. Sadness softened his expression. But when he met Tyler's eyes again, his own were hard as glass.

"I'm sorry, Tyler," he said. "I know you won't believe me, but I am."

He lifted the gun. Tyler tensed.

Then came a thump and a confused noise. Tyler forced his eyes open, not realizing he'd shut them. Damon was gone.

Tyler scanned the shadows, his heart pounding. There was a dull scuffling noise, a strangled cry. He ran toward the sound.

He could make out a figure thrashing on the ground. No, two figures, grappling, one making strangled noises.

"Lucien, *stop*."

Lucien went still. Slowly, he sat up. Damon was sprawled on the ground under him, feebly struggling. The gun lay in the grass nearby.

The blood on Lucien's mouth and chin looked black in the starlight. Tyler fought the urge to back away.

"Let him go."

"He was going to kill you." The way his blood-covered mouth moved was eerie. His eyes were red pits in the shadows of his face.

"He's not worth it," Tyler breathed.

"*You* are," Lucien insisted. He bent over Damon. Tyler grabbed his shoulders.

"Please," he begged. "This isn't the answer."

Lucien paused. Damon shivered and twitched on the ground, making wet, choked noises. His blood soaked the grass. His face in the moonlight was sick and pale, his eyes wide.

"Lucien," Tyler said again, his voice catching in his throat.

Lucien straightened. He gazed up at Tyler. His face looked ghastly, blood-streaked and pale, his eyes glowing like hot coals. His fingers were dug into Damon's flesh. He opened his mouth to speak, his fangs glinting in the moonlight.

The wail of a siren made Tyler jump. Brakes screeched. Blue lights flashed.

"Shit," Tyler swore, heart climbing into his throat. "Lucien, go."

Lucien didn't move.

"Lucien," Tyler said, grabbing him and trying to drag him off Damon.

"No," he said, shrugging off Tyler's hold, standing and squaring his shoulders. His face was resolute.

"If they catch you like this," Tyler said, shoving him with all his strength but Lucien was unmovable as stone, "every nutter in the country will be out with pitchforks and stakes."

"I'm not afraid to face judgment. Some might say it's long overdue."

"Think, will you?" Tyler begged. "If not for yourself then for the rest of us."

Lucien frowned faintly.

"Remember what I thought last time, huh?" he whispered. "And people like me? Remember what we did to Emory when we thought he'd kidnapped that kid? They'll go after him again, Lucien. And the others. I was wrong about Emory, Lucien. I know I was. Maybe I was wrong about all of you." Something shifted in Lucien's eyes. He visibly paled. Tyler swallowed. "If you won't do it for me, do it for him — for Emory, for his family."

Commotion could be heard inside the pub. Tyler glanced over his shoulder as the door opened. When he looked back, Lucien was gone.

Damon still lay spread-eagled on the grass with his eyes wide open. There was so much blood. Tyler couldn't tell if he was breathing. He knelt to check with his head spinning. Rough hands grabbed him from behind.

"Tyler Lomax, you are under arrest…"

He didn't hear the rest. Damon wasn't breathing.

\* \* \* \*

"That lawyer is still waiting in reception, Tyler. Are you sure you don't want him in here?"

Tyler wished they'd open a window. The interview room was even stuffier than last time. His clothes smelled stale, and Damon's blood was drying brown on his shirt and jeans. He refused to meet DI Walker's gaze.

"Are you absolutely certain?" the detective asked, yet again. "I'm no fashion expert, but I can tell his shoes cost more than I make in a month. I'm guessing that means he's a very good lawyer."

"I don't want a lawyer."

"Your sister won't be happy about that," put in the petite detective constable sat at Walker's left. Her eyes were on her notepad, and she scribbled as she spoke.

Tyler didn't reply.

"Fine," Walker said, straightening in his chair. "No lawyer." The detective's shirt was rumpled, his tie loose under his collar. The heat in the room was making beads of sweat appear at his hairline. There were shadows under his amber eyes, but his gaze was alert and locked on Tyler. "I need you to tell me what happened," he said, "for your own sake. The victim was clearly stabbed. But there were no weapons of that kind found at the scene. Only the gun. And the only fingerprints on that gun belonged to the victim."

Tyler stared at the table even harder.

"The medical report says he has suffered exsanguination," Walker said quietly. "Very similar to our visitors that arrived the same morning you did. Remember?"

That incident felt like so long ago it was like another lifetime. Tyler groped after the feelings from that day — the anger, the hot fear. But all there was was emptiness.

"We know you didn't *bite* anyone, Tyler," Walker said, his voice low and hard. "But we know you know who did."

"If you know so much, what do you need me for?"

Walker sighed and flipped open his notebook. "Talk to me about the victim, then. Who is he?"

"Ask him yourself."

"He's not talking, either," Walker said, tapping his pen off the notebook. "Two of a kind, you two, you could say."

"I'm nothing like him."

"He has the excuse of a wound near his vocal cords and an illegal firearm he's reluctant to explain," Walker said. "He's protecting himself. Who are you protecting?"

Tyler felt sick. He glared to stop anything showing in his face.

Walker opened a file and laid out several photographs. They were from Damon's compound — the empty building above ground, the living area, the room containing Lucien's sleeping cell, the observation room, the wall of weapons.

"Still think you don't need that lawyer?" the constable asked.

Tyler's blood had drained from his head, leaving him sick and dizzy.

"We know you were there, Tyler," Walker said quietly. "Your fingerprints and, well…" — Walker raised an eyebrow — "let's just call it DNA, are everywhere."

"I—" Tyler said through clenched teeth. "I wasn't…"

Walker watched him closely. "The place has cameras, Tyler. Lots of them."

Tyler swallowed bile.

"If you already know everything," he managed to say, "just charge me and get it over with."

Walker slid his constable a glance. She took a breath and sat forward.

"Our arrival at the location triggered some sort of wipe of the security system," she said cautiously. "But our tech department is very good. They've already retrieved some footage."

She laid more photos on the table — stills of Damon and Tyler arriving, them in the observation room, watching. Tyler's guts filled with ice as she withdrew another.

It was Lucien. He stood in the white room, staring at the one-way mirror, his face rigid.

"This is your last chance to help yourself," DI Walker said. "Tell me what is going on in these pictures. Tell me what you and your friend are doing with this haemophile."

"He's not my friend," Tyler snapped, slamming his hand over the image of Lucien. "He's a crazy arsehole. He deserved what he got."

Walker folded his arms and studied Tyler. Tyler tried to slow his breathing but couldn't look away.

"We have photographic evidence of you kidnapping this haemophile and other evidence of illegal experimentation and torture. This is serious shit, Tyler."

Tyler's jaw ached. He dug his fingernails into his palms, but he refused to break eye contact. "So...charge me."

The constable narrowed her eyes. Walker leaned on the table.

"Bottom line, Tyler." Walker tapped the image of Damon. "This is the man we're interested in. We don't know his name, but we have evidence linking him to other crimes, other suspects. All of them are very nasty people who do very nasty things. So far, we haven't gathered anything concrete enough to launch a formal investigation. You could give us our starting point...unless you're one of them?"

"Like hell."

"Well, then?" Walker pointed at Damon's picture. "Who is this man?"

"Ask *him*," he said, voice strained. "Ask him all this shit. I'm done with it. All of it."

"It's too late for that," Walker said in a low voice. He pushed the photo of Lucien toward him. "This is Lucien, isn't it? The haemophile that attacked you on the moor?"

Tyler bit the inside of his mouth. The picture blurred before his eyes.

"You decided to take matters into your own hands, is that right?"

"No, I…" Tyler made a noise then covered his mouth.

"It's all here in high definition," the constable said quietly. "It's only a matter of time before the tech guys retrieve more. There will be footage of what you actually *did* to this haemophile while he was your prisoner."

"No," Tyler shook his head vehemently. "I didn't hurt him. I would never hurt him."

There was a long, full silence. The police officers exchanged glances, but Tyler was too dizzy to figure out what they might mean.

"He could hurt *you*," Walker said, producing a picture of a pale and bloody Damon on a stretcher. "Was this him, Tyler? Was this Lucien?"

Tyler took a deep shuddering breath. "It's my fault," he whispered. "It's all my fault." He looked Walker in the eye. "I wanted Lucien. I hired that psycho to help me find him. And it's my fault that this all happened." He swallowed, his throat thick and tight. "Charge me."

Walker examined him for a long time then sighed and began to gather the pictures.

"Take him to the custody sergeant, Vickers," he said, standing.

"Wait," Tyler said, getting shakily to his feet. "I told you to charge me."

"Maybe in the morning," Walker said flatly. "This is not just about you, Tyler. There's a bigger picture here, and I think, given a chance to reflect, you'll realize that."

The prison cell was gloomy and smelled like piss and bleach, but at least the concrete walls made it fractionally cooler than the rest of the police station. Tyler lay on the hard bunk and stared at the ceiling. His body ached, like someone had taken each of his muscles and yanked them, hard. His heart slugged a dull rhythm in his chest. The air was heavy in his throat and seemed to clog his lungs.

Images of Lucien, of Damon, of blood, of torture instruments and of strangers cleaning guns all rose one after another before his eyes then sloughed away like waste down a drain.

He tried to remember the last time he'd been certain, the last time he remembered exactly who he was and what he wanted. All that came to him was the sound of Lucien's voice, the feel and taste of his skin, the sensation of his powerful body yielding to Tyler's like it had been built for that sole purpose.

But then he'd attacked Damon. And he couldn't forget the list. The length of it. No matter how evil his victims were, he'd still killed them...all of them. Tore their throats open and drunk their blood. Hidden their bodies. Lived hundreds of years without facing consequences.

*I can't change my nature any more than you could.*

He covered his face in his hands. He just wanted it all to end. All of it.

"I'm sorry, Tyler."

Tyler jerked upright. Night had fallen. The room was thick with shadows. Lucien stepped into the thin moonlight leaking in through the barred window.

For a second all Tyler could do was draw his breath in and out.

"Lucien?"

Lucien moved closer. Tyler stood. Lucien gazed into Tyler's face. His chest loosened. His body no longer hurt. He let his hands hover over Lucien's shoulders but didn't dare touch.

"Are you really here?"

Lucien blinked. His eyes were shining. "I shouldn't have done this to you."

"Done what?"

"Any of it," Lucien whispered. "I shouldn't have touched you that day at Emory's. I shouldn't have encouraged your feelings after that. I know better."

"I'm the one who's sorry," Tyler said. "If I'd just left you alone… If I'd just let this whole thing go back then…"

"I'd still be out there," Lucien cut him off. "Biting. Killing." Lucien raised one shoulder in a defeated shrug. "You helped me understand myself, Tyler. I'll always be grateful to you for that. I know what I have to do now. I just hope it's not too late for you."

"Too late for what?" Tyler's voice sounded strange in his own ears. Lucien's words held such a dreadful finality. He both needed and really didn't want an answer.

Lucien's expression softened. He ran his fingers up Tyler's arms and interlaced them behind his neck and pulled him down.

The kiss was slow but intense, a blaze contained in a furnace, a storm waiting in a cloud. Tyler drank in Lucien's heady, autumnal taste. He slid his hands around his hips and drew him close. Everything else fell away. All that mattered was the Lucien in his arms, the taste of his mouth, the low sounds of his growing arousal.

"I love you," Tyler breathed, breaking the kiss to bury his face in Lucien's neck. "Fuck, I love you, Lucien."

Lucien sighed, deep and slow, ran his hands up Tyler's back and tilted his face to murmur into his ear.

"Tyler…"

The cell door opening jerked Tyler to wakefulness like a bucket of cold water.

He blinked blearily and sat up. The light in the room was the dull gray of dawn.

DC Vickers stood in the doorway with her hands in her trouser pockets and a strained expression.

"Wakey, wakey, sunshine. Time to go."

"Huh?" he grumbled groggily.

She jerked her thumb out the door. "Go on. Off you pop."

"I don't get it."

She made an impatient noise. "I'm telling you to get gone. *Now*. Charges have been dropped."

"What? Why?"

"Above my pay grade, mate. Now bugger off. We need the cell."

"Where's Walker?"

She gave him a baleful look in answer.

Tyler drifted from the cell in a daze. The brightness of the corridor made him blink. He frowned when the constable turned left down the hall, instead of right toward the lobby and the exit. She took him along several anonymous corridors to a fire exit, shoved the release bar and pushed it open.

He stepped out into the narrow alley that was already close and hot in the rising sun. Emerald stood there in a bottle-green dress with her arms folded and a hard look on her face. She was tapping her patent shoe impatiently on the rubbish-strewn cobbles.

"All yours, Mayor," the DC said with a snide smile and shut the door with a bang.

"Emmy? What the — ?"

"Not here," she said, turned on her heel and strode away. He followed her to her black car where her driver held open the back door. Tyler just caught a glimpse of the crowd gathered on the police station steps before he climbed inside.

Tyler sank into the seat and covered his face in his hands as the car pulled away.

"Okay, Tyler," Emerald said in a low, hard voice. "This is the part where you tell me everything."

Tyler dropped his hands. "I didn't ask you to help me," he muttered.

"I didn't help, did I?" she snapped. "I tried, but you wouldn't let me." She was staring ahead, her manicured fingers interwoven so tightly in her lap her fingertips were going pale. "Do you have any idea how much that lawyer charged me just to sit in the lobby while you refused to see him?"

"I told you," Tyler said, sitting up. "I didn't ask for help."

"You don't have to bloody ask, do you? That's the point of family, dickhead." She cleared her throat, sneaking him a glance then looking away again. "Not that it was any bloody use. Are you an idiot or what?"

"How much of an idiot do *you* have to be to get me off these bloody charges when you're about to run in an election?"

She looked at him narrowly. "I didn't get you off."

Tyler blinked. "You didn't?"

"No."

"Then who did?"

"Do you have any idea how worried I've been?" she said after a heavy pause. "You just vanished, Tyler. Up and left. No texts. Nothing. And after all that shit that went on with Fleetwood and all those other guys?" Her face flushed pink. "I thought you were dead, you arsehole."

Tyler slouched in his seat.

"None of that," she said, shoving his arm. "We're not kids anymore. Stop sulking and start talking."

# Chapter Nine

Tyler told her everything — about the phone number Brandon gave him, hiring Damon, finding Lucien's hide. Running away to The Fort.

"He took you...where?" The look on his sister's face was strained.

"Some sort of weird clubhouse," Tyler murmured. "Full of these weirdos...with weapons, guns."

"A club for vampire hunters?" Tyler nodded. "Jesus."

"It's my fault," Tyler said, shaking his head. "I hired him. I slept with him."

"You...you *what*?"

"I was scared and horny, okay?" Tyler snapped. "I didn't know what I wanted. Story of my bloody life. I thought I wanted to —"

"You're a bloody idiot, Tyler," Emerald snapped. "I've told you before and I'm telling you again. I *told* you not to get involved with these people. What were you thinking?"

"I wasn't, was I?" he cried. His face was hot. His skin was itchy all over. "I wasn't bloody thinking. I never bloody think. I thought Damon could fix it all. I thought I could make it all right again. I didn't realize there was nothing *to* fix. And now..."

Emerald took a breath then took his hand. "And now?"

"And now I love him. I'm fucking terrified of him, but I love him."

"Damon?"

Tyler grimaced. "Not Damon."

Emerald paled. "Lucien?"

Tyler opened and closed his mouth, made a noise and buried his head in his hands.

"Tyler, we gotta get you to a shrink or something," Emerald said, her tone dull with shock. "This is clearly some sort of PTSD."

"It's not," Tyler insisted. "I want it to be, but it's not."

"You don't know that."

"I *do* know that. Because now I know this is what it was all about from the start." He looked his sister in the eye. "I wasn't scared of Lucien because I thought he might kill me. I was scared of Lucien because I was going mad for him and didn't have the first damn clue how to handle it."

Emerald stared at him.

"You know I'm telling the truth. When have I ever been this messed up about a guy, ever?"

"Oh, baby brother," she said, her voice thick with swallowed tears. "How did this happen?"

"I don't know," he choked. "I don't fall for people. It's not how I do things. I just don't..." He shook his head. "Men aren't worth it."

"Some are."

He looked at her. She was giving him a wan smile. But then it fell away. "So what happened?"

Tyler scowled. "Damon wanted information from him—about people he'd killed, where he'd hidden them, unregistered hides—"

"What?"

"Secret places haemophiles have to run to when they need to. Places where they're safe."

"I don't understand. All their communes are registered."

"These are off the books," Tyler said softly. "Ones we don't know about. That's the only way they stay safe."

Emerald's face clouded.

"Damon was gonna find all that out then he was gonna kill him." Tyler stared hard at the ceiling. "*We* were gonna kill him."

"Tyler..."

"No, I have to say it," Tyler snapped. "I have to get it out." He took a breath. "We were gonna kill him...together. That was the whole point of all of it. I knew it, knew it but didn't. I had thought I was fixing everything. Until..."—he drew a shaking breath—"I couldn't do it."

A pause. "So, what did you do?"

"I helped him escape. He took me with him." He sat up, glowering at the frosted screen that separated them from the driver. They were heading along Fishergate toward the city center. The buildings looked different, somehow, like he was seeing them for the first time. "We hid for a couple of days, staying out of Damon's way while Lucien got his strength back. That's why you didn't hear from me. I couldn't give us away."

"Hid where?"

"I'm not supposed to say. But, honestly, I couldn't tell you if I wanted to. Somewhere at the arse end of nowhere." He chewed his lip. "We talked. We—" He winced. "You know. But we talked, too. Really talked." He looked up. "I've never talked to anyone like that before, Emmy. I've never felt like I could admit all the worst parts of me like that. He understood them…understood me."

Emerald drew her eyebrows together. "You can talk to me, Tyler…always."

He shook his head. "Not about this stuff."

"You really think there's anything about you I don't already know?"

"I would bet on it."

"Tyler," she said, taking his hand, pulling it into her lap and laying the other hand over the top. Her skin was warm, her grip firm. "I know you think you're a monster, but you're not. You're a good man. An angry one"—she squeezed his hand—"but not a bad one. You're not Dad."

He wanted to snatch his hand back, but he couldn't. He couldn't look away from her face.

"Lucien said something like that, too," he whispered. "And I think he could make me believe it."

"If he's worth all this," she said. "I bloody hope so."

Tyler dropped his gaze to the floor.

"So," she said, drawing a deep breath. "You're in this place, hiding out, talking…and a whole lot more," she said, her tone changed. Tyler felt himself blush but didn't look up. "Then you're being arrested in a pub car park over a half-dead vampire hunter."

"It's fucked," Tyler whispered. "It's all *so* fucked."

"What happened?"

"I don't even know," Tyler said. "Lucien was gonna leave, get the hell away. But the haemos tried to deal with him, then Damon caught up with me. Maybe he'd put a trace on my phone and when I'd powered it on, he found me. He had a gun." Tyler raised his eyes. "We were so close. He was going to run, leave all the biting and vigilante shit behind."

"So he really did go after those men because they were creeps?"

Tyler nodded. "He's been doing it forever—hunting evil people, like some sort of immortal superhero." He looked at the ceiling. "Only he kills them."

Emerald was very still. "He didn't kill Fleetwood… or the other three."

"He came close," Tyler whispered. "And given another chance, he still might. So…" He heaved a sigh. "I convinced him to leave. It was the only thing we could think of to break the cycle."

"He was going to leave? And not see you again?"

He swallowed. "Yeah."

"And you were okay with that?"

"I dunno," Tyler rasped. "Honestly, I hadn't thought past getting him away."

"And you? What were you gonna do?"

"Well, that's why I rang you, wasn't it? I knew I had to get home to try to get ahead of all this. But then Damon showed up, then the bloody cops…"

Emerald's expression had fallen. She let go of his hand.

Heat swelled in Tyler's chest. "*You* sent the cops?"

"What was I supposed to do?" she snapped. "You call out of the blue after days of nothing then the call cuts like that. I thought you were in trouble. You *were* in trouble."

"But now the cops have Damon," Tyler said, his palms sweating. "Damon with a bloody hole in his neck. Damon, who already wanted Lucien dead, and Christ only knows what he'll do now."

"He can't do anything while the cops have him. Think straight, Tyler. If the man really is what you say he is, he's getting stuck somewhere where the sun don't shine for a long time."

"But it's not just *him*. He's got that whole network of lunatics. All he needs to do is get the word out—"

"So, what, Tyler? What do you want me to do? Take you back to Walker?" She snorted. "If you'd wanted to stop Damon's mates, you would have talked to Walker."

"I just wanted to protect Lucien," he said, his voice losing power. They'd pulled up outside Tyler's apartment building. The strength had bled out of him, and he slumped in his seat. He just wanted to close his eyes and disappear. "All I was thinking about was Lucien—about what I did to him—kidnapping him, drugging him, planning to kill him. I wanted to be punished for that." He rolled his head on the headrest to look at his sister. "I should be in jail, before I do anything else stupid."

Emerald heaved a large sigh. "Well, you're not, so deal with it. *Make* something out of all this."

Tyler's ire rose, swelled then died. "Like what?"

His sister looked at him closely. "Think about what matters, Tyler. Really matters. Then you'll know."

Tyler put his hand on the door handle but didn't open it. "I shouldn't be free," he whispered. "Why am I?"

Emerald was quiet. The air conditioning hummed. The traffic rolled by outside. The sun was high and bright in the sky.

Tyler made himself wait quietly, even though his grip on the door handle was tight enough to hurt.

"My contacts could only tell me some of it."

"Some of *what*?"

She looked at him. "Lucien turned himself in just before dawn."

It was like the car was rocking. His muscles tensed and his stomach rolled. "*What?*"

"He presented himself at Fulford Road. He spoke to DI Walker. He admitted to attacking Damon and those other men. He also said that he had gone to that compound place voluntarily and that you had nothing to do with keeping him there—or with anything else that Damon did."

"Why?" Tyler breathed. "Why would he do that?"

"You were about to take the blame for everything. Apparently, he wanted to do the same and was more convincing." Emerald's expression softened. She leaned over him and opened the car door. Warm air flooded the car. "Go, Tyler. Take a shower. Get some rest. It will all make sense tomorrow."

Tyler blinked until his body finally caught up with his brain. "You gotta help him," he said, grabbing Emerald's arm. "Please. You gotta get him off."

"I can't do that, Tyler. I couldn't even get you off, remember?"

"That was just because I'm your brother. It would be too obvious. No one knows you have a link to Lucien. You could get him off without it ever getting back to you. I know you could. You can do anything."

Emerald looked pained. "I'm flattered you think so, little brother. But calling in a favor to have you brought out the back of the station isn't the same as getting a haemophile off assault and murder charges."

"You got me brought out the back for *you*," Tyler said through gritted teeth. "Do this for *me*."

Emerald's face darkened. "Go home, Tyler. Sleep. When you're thinking straight, you can see you're talking crazy."

"I've never been more sane."

"You think Lucien was kept in a regular police cell like you?" she snapped. "Of course not. Walker handed him over to the goons from the International Assembly for Haemophile Affairs. This goes way, way above my head…and Walker's. Lucien's gone. It's over."

"No," Tyler said, voice breaking. "He can't. He wouldn't."

"He did," Emerald said firmly. "And he did it for you, so don't make it for nothing. Go home. Figure out a way to get through this. And don't screw up your second chance. You won't get another one."

Tyler stepped out of the car into the heat of the sun. Instantly people surrounded him, holding recording devices and phone cameras to his face.

"Tyler Lomax, what can you tell us about the haemophile attack in Illington? Did he assault you, too? How many people has he killed, Tyler?"

Tyler forced his way through, got the front door of the building open and slammed it in their faces.

His phone was ringing when he took it out of his pocket. There were already dozens of missed calls from unknown numbers. His landline was ringing, too.

He yanked it out of the wall.

He went to the bathroom, stripped off his dirty and blood-spattered clothes and turned the shower to its hottest setting. His skin was flushed red in seconds. He stuck his head under the spray and rubbed his hands through his matted hair, raking the shampoo through it, scrubbing hard — but the feelings didn't wash away.

He lay on his bed naked, the window open, the bright sunshine and car fumes filling the air. The familiar walls and pictures, like the buildings outside, all felt different, like he was apart from them, living in darkness, even in the middle of the day. It no longer felt like home. He wondered if it ever had.

He closed his eyes and willed Lucien to come to him, like he had before. Had they been dreams? Hallucinations? Or had he really been there? Haemophiles could do all sorts of weird things. Get into locked rooms. Vanish again without a trace.

Maybe it had all been real.

Yes, in that moment, he was certain it had all been real.

Tyler opened his eyes and stared at the ceiling. *So why would he throw it all away?*

He grabbed his phone. He searched every article and news clip. The story was everywhere.

*Haemophile murderer caught.*

*Heamophile confesses to assault charges.*

*Nameless haemophile to face charges at the International Haemophile Court of Justice.*

There were photos and videos of Tyler's arrest, footage of him being bundled into a police car outside the Fox and Hounds. There were other pictures, too, lifted from his social media pages. Here he was grinning at the York Races or sitting behind the wheel of the Ferrari he'd hired to race around Monte Carlo with Brandon. There was information on the property portfolio their crooked politician father had left them, reports of his previous arrests and acquittals, Emerald's links to both and more on his suspected involvement in the violent protests outside Emory Von Magnusson's house during his custody case.

Some posts declared him as a hate criminal and an entitled bigot. Others hailed him as a hero and visionary, someone not afraid to speak out against the clear threat haemophiles presented to society.

Tyler felt unsteady, like the ground was about to give way. Everything he'd tried to decide, tried to figure out or spent his life running away from was spelled out in black and white, all over the internet.

He scrolled on, his mouth dry and head spinning.

Finally, he found it. It was a post on a gossip forum. A conspiracy chat room, really. But the theory seemed to come up more than once, and the people on there seemed to have more info than many of the journalists releasing the official reports.

*He's being held in the holding facility in London.*

*They say it's under the Old Bailey.*

*They always said there were secret chambers under there, and now we know…*

He didn't read the rest of the thread. He dialed a number and paced the room.

"Tyler?"

"Naz, I need help."

Silence answered him.

Tyler sighed. "Naz, I know, it's official. I'm a 24-carat, prize-winning arsehole. I will say sorry when I can, when I've got time to do it right. But in the meantime, I need a favor."

"Seriously?"

Tyler sat on the edge of his bed. He made himself take several breaths before speaking further. "Naz, please. I'm a dick but you're not. You're one of the best people I know." He swallowed emotion and stared at the ceiling. "I was an idiot for screwing it up with you. But you were too good for me. You gotta see that?"

"Goodbye, Tyler."

"No, wait, please," Tyler begged. "I'll try to make it up to you when my head isn't up my arse. But please. If I ever meant anything to you, can you do this one thing for me?"

Another paused. Tyler made himself wait, biting his lip.

"You want to see him, don't you? Lucien? You two are a thing now?"

Tyler almost dropped the phone. He gathered himself and steadied his voice. "How did you know?"

"Tyler, please. I knew before you did. Remember? I told you to face the truth, and you'd feel better. I must confess, I didn't expect you to try to hunt the truth down like a wild animal and get arrested in the process. Tell me, do you ever think with the organ actually *meant* for thinking?"

"Naz," Tyler pleaded.

A loud sigh on the other end of the phone. "What do you think I can do?"

Tyler took a breath. "He's being held in some specialist place, in London?"

"I know the one," Nasir said quietly. "I still have my friends from law school working the departments down there."

"Yeah, I remember you'd mentioned having friends in these places. So you can get me in, right?"

"There are no visiting hours in that facility, Tyler," Nasir said wryly. "It's top-level security clearance. Not even the prime minister could visit if his haemophile boyfriend was being held there."

Tyler clutched the covers. "He's doing all this for me. He's gonna go to prison to save me. I can't let him do it. I have to speak to him. I *have* to."

A pause. "I'll make some calls...maybe at least confirm that's where he is. But I can't promise anything."

"Thank you," Tyler said, words coming out in a rush. "Thank you, Naz, thank you."

"Don't thank me, Tyler," he said harshly. "All I'm saying it that I'll ask the questions."

Tyler started to thank him again, but he'd hung up.

Time slowed to a crawl. Tyler paced between the windows and the living room. He tried to eat but didn't manage more than half a cheese sandwich. The buzzer for the apartment building started going non-stop. He went to the window. The crowd on the pavement had grown. He swore, closed all the windows, drew all the curtains and pulled the doorbell out of the wall.

The light dimmed. Every time he turned on the TV, the reports were still streaming, but there was no new news.

DI Walker tried to phone him, but he ignored the call. The guy left a voicemail.

Tyler's palms itched as he imagined all the things Walker could potentially be ringing to say. Finally, he caved and pressed play.

*"Tyler, it's me. Perhaps you'll believe me now when I say you won't go down for any of this. Why not come in and talk to me? Help me take this haemophile hate group down. You know you have nothing to lose. A* pause. *You have a chance to do a good thing here. It's too late for Lucien, but you can make the world safer for others like him. Please. Ring me back."*

Tyler stared at the phone for a long time then deleted the message.

He cracked a curtain and stared out at the sky, holding his breath as the sun set. His automatic lamps flickered on, but he stayed at the window, staring out. When it was fully dark, he drifted back to his couch. He sat. He waited.

Nothing happened.

When the phone rang, he almost dropped it before he could answer, his hands were shaking so badly.

"Naz?"

"I'm sorry, Tyler."

"No," Tyler cut him off. "No, don't be sorry. Tell me you sorted it."

"I couldn't."

"But you said," he said, tears choking his voice. "You said you knew people."

"I do. But all I said I could do was ask them. The prison doesn't even officially exist. I may have a law degree, but I'm just a PA to the Mayor of York. I can tell you he's there, but I can't —"

Tyler hung up the phone. He lay on the sofa with his arms over his head.

He jerked in surprise when the doorbell rang. For several moments he lay there, confused. Then he realized it wasn't the bell for the door to the building. It was for his own front door. He lay very still, wondering if he'd imagined it. But then it rang again.

He lifted his phone and tapped the app for the video feed. Three figures stood in the hall. One was Jesse Truelove. His expression was serious. Next to him was his fiancé, the Baron Emory Von Magnusson. As distracting as Jesse was, the tall and broad-shouldered haemophile with eyes of the deepest and darkest blue Tyler had ever seen took his breath away — and not in a good way. Tyler was catapulted back to the woods, with the ring of haemophiles around him, Magnusson's penetrating gaze locked on Lucien.

His face was as unreadable in the hall light as it had been out in the moonless night, but the bottomless gaze still made him feel like he was adrift at sea and drowning.

At his shoulder stood Darragh Kelly. Seeing him in the light made Tyler's blood slow with fear. He was dressed in a pinstripe suit and tie, despite the heat that had yet to fade, and his eyes were as sharp as cut glass.

Tyler somehow made it to the door and opened it. With all three of their gazes landing on him at once, his whole body chilled. He attempted to shut the door again, but Jesse got his foot in.

"We just want to talk."

"I can't handle this right now," Tyler said, staring at Jesse's chest rather than at anyone's face.

"Tyler." Magnusson's voice was kind but firm.

Tyler hesitated then stepped back. The three came inside, the haemophiles moving on soundless feet. Jesse hovered in the doorway with him, his eyes bright with uncertainty. But then he laid a hand on Tyler's arm.

The contact went through him like an electric shock but then settled and warmed him under his quaking stomach. His breathing slowed. He found he was able to close the door and follow Jesse to the living room. The two haemophiles were standing in the middle of the room, motionless and looking expectantly at Tyler as Jesse wandered around, taking in the room.

"Mr. Lomax," Kelly said, his soft Irish accent curving the sharpness of the words, "it's very nice to see you again. Though I'm sorry it is under such circumstances."

"I told you," he said in a low voice, staring at the lawyer's shoes, "this is not a good time."

"That's what we want to talk to you about," Magnusson said. Tyler raised his eyes. The haemophile gestured at the couch. "May we?"

Tyler hesitated, then nodded stiffly. Magnusson sat. Jesse sat next to him and took his hand, apparently without thinking. Their engagement rings glinted in the lamplight. Jesse looked hard at Tyler. Kelly stayed standing, scrutinizing him with an unreadable look on his fine-boned face.

Tyler moved to a chair and sat. "Well? What do you want?"

"We've always wanted what you want," Magnusson said after a long, strained silence. "Lucien safe."

"It didn't sound like you wanted him safe" Tyler replied, glaring at them each in turn. "You wanted him out of the way, like everyone else does. He doesn't fit your plan, so you want him gone."

"You can drop the act, Tyler," Jesse said softly. "I know you're not as big of a prick as you like people to think you are."

"You don't know anything about me."

"I know you did everything you did because you were angry," Jesse said smoothly. "Pretending you wanted what I wanted that night in the Evil Eye then pretending you hated Emory, throwing rocks at his house."

Tyler suddenly found it hard to meet Jesse's gaze.

"I know a little bit about being ashamed of your needs," Jesse continued softly. "And I think you've realized, now, that everything is so much easier when you admit the truth."

"Jesse's right, Tyler," Magnusson said quietly. "And maybe you're right, too. Maybe we didn't handle things well, out there in the woods. But we've been here before. We thought we knew how to manage Lucien, how to protect him from himself."

"You don't know anything about him," Tyler ground out. "You think you do, but you don't. If you knew him like I do, you would never have ditched him."

Jesse tensed, but Magnusson squeezed his hand, not taking his eyes off Tyler. "I still care about him. We all do."

"So why don't you help him, huh?" he snapped. "You let him think that turning himself in was his only choice."

"We have monitored Lucien for hundreds of years," Kelly said. "We know what he does, what drives him.

He has to be handled carefully. And for a long time, he has been quiet."

"Quiet?"

"Lucien protects himself and your kind by avoiding you," Magnusson said. "For years at a time...centuries, sometimes. He knows what he does is unacceptable... medieval."

"He does what he thinks is right," Tyler said.

Magnusson inclined his head. "He does. But he also knows there is no place for it in the world anymore. To cope with this, he isolates himself. But with the population of the world being what it is, that is harder than it used to be. So he gets drawn back. He almost can't help himself. So when he does surface, we monitor him."

"He's not a convict out on parole," Tyler muttered. "You should help him change. If you treat him like a fugitive on the run, he'll act like one."

"We do what we do for the best interests of all," Magnusson said calmly. "We do it to avoid exactly what has happened to him now."

Tyler looked at the floor. His blood pounded in his temples, making it hard for him to concentrate.

"Emory doesn't blame you," Jesse said, his voice harder. "I do. But he doesn't."

Tyler glowered at Jesse. Jesse's only response was to raise an eyebrow. Magnusson was calm, his eyes again deep and blank.

"No one can make Lucien do anything he doesn't want to do," Magnusson said. "If he's handed himself in, it's because he wanted to. I just want to understand why now, after all this time."

Tyler made a frustrated noise. He stood and faced the wall, chewing the side of his thumb. "Because of me."

"Pardon?" Magnusson asked.

"Because of me, all right?" Tyler said, louder. "I kidnapped him. Held him captive. I did all that horrible shit. But then I fell in love with him — and I think he did with me. Then it was all about to come out, everything I'd done, so he threw himself to the wolves…to save me."

"You don't kidnap someone you love," Jesse muttered.

"You do if you're messed up," Tyler said, turning back, his voice cracking. "If you're a fuck-up. If you have no idea what you want or how to handle it when you get it. If you're so used to fucking up every good thing that comes into your life that the only thing you can do to someone who makes you feel anything is to hurt them — or want them to hurt you."

Jesse's face paled. Magnusson gave him a quiet, intimate smile and patted his hand. Jesse looked away.

Tyler glanced at Kelly, standing watchful and silent, his keen, green eyes on Tyler.

"Lucien admitted to attacking those men," Tyler continued in a hoarse voice. "And told them he'd gone to the place we held him voluntarily. He said I had nothing to do with what Damon did — or wanted to do."

"Damon?" Kelly said, his eyes keen.

Tyler rubbed his face. "The hunter I hired. The one he nearly killed."

Jesse made a noise, but Magnusson put his hand on his knee. He fell quiet again.

"It's like I said," Kelly said. "Emory? I said all this. I said they were out there, these groups. That they were growing more bold."

"Did you tell the police about Damon, Tyler?" Magnusson asked.

Tyler hesitated. There was no judgment in Magnusson's tone or his face. He was terrifying to look at, but somehow Tyler's fear wasn't about that right now. He swallowed.

"No."

"Why not?" Magnusson asked.

"I don't care about any of that," Tyler said. "Not about Damon. Not about the others like him. All I care about is Lucien."

"If you cared about Lucien, you'd talk to the police," Jesse said firmly.

"DI Walker's already tried that line on me, Truelove," Tyler bit out. "So save it."

"What will it take, Tyler?" Jesse said. His face had changed. His tone was pleading. "What else will it take for humans to realize we need to *do* something? Do something to make all this easier?"

"I. Don't. Care," Tyler said. "The world is full of shit people doing shit things — human, haemophile, whatever. I don't want any part of it. I never have. Lucien is the only thing I ever wanted to be in with. Okay, so I wasn't smart enough to know how to handle that to start. But I am now. I don't care about any of the rest of it. Only him." He took a shaking breath, got himself under control. "And now he's going to prison. And there's nothing left to care about."

Silence stretched between them for a long time. Then, finally, Kelly stepped forward.

"Which brings us to why we're here," he said. He put his hands in his pockets and put his head on one side. "Lucien is refusing to put in a defense. He's refusing to even take any legal advice. He knows it could affect the future of all haemophiles who get accused of violence against humans, but he won't acknowledge the reality of the situation. A bit like yourself."

"Why should he?" Tyler muttered. He blinked away tears. "It's too late to fight."

"Not true," Magnusson said quietly. "Darragh thinks there's hope."

Something in Tyler's chest loosened. "There is?"

"Not if he won't talk to me," Kelly said. He took a seat on the other chair, crossing his legs and folding his hands in his lap as casually as if they were all about to play a game of cards.

*Bloody lawyers*, Tyler thought, but kept his mouth shut.

"Lucien thinks the laws of today to be infantile and below his interest, and the Lord Above knows I've been practicing law long enough to agree with him, to a certain extent. But what I know better than him is the fact that, infantile or not, they will dictate what happens to him next—which could be anything from centuries of imprisonment to execution."

"Execution?" Tyler barked, his blood chilling in his veins.

"The International Haemophile Court of Justice is very new," Kelly put in ominously. "We used to police things ourselves. We know we can no longer do that." He sent a hard look at Magnusson, as if repeating a discussion they'd already had. "So we have to support this new court. But the laws are altering all the time to adapt to new circumstances. The campaign for extermination of haemophile criminals has been around for as long as we've been out of hiding. Longer, even. For as long as we've existed there have been people wanting us gone from the world." Kelly narrowed his gaze and crossed his legs the other way. "And now the idea's gathering support from powerful people. Lucien's case is just the sort of thing they've been waiting for—brutal violence, historical crimes, a confession. This is a dream to them."

"So what are you gonna do about it?" Tyler demanded. "You're a lawyer. Fix it."

Kelly regarded him levelly. "I told you. He won't talk to me." He paused for a moment. "But maybe you can change his mind?"

Tyler blinked, thoughts chasing themselves round his brain.

"It was clear how you felt about each other in the woods," Magnusson said. "I've never seen or heard him act like that—not for a haemophile, not for a human, no one."

"You can do it, Tyler," Jesse said. "Get him to talk to Kelly. If he cares about you like you say, he'll do it."

"Why do you care?" he whispered. "Why do any of you care? You hate him."

"We don't hate him," Magnusson said, calmly and softly but with tremendous weight behind the words. "We care about him. All of us do."

"Because of this weird bond you have?" The jealousy was real and ugly in that moment, and Tyler couldn't fight it long enough to keep the words unsaid. Jesse looked uncertain, glancing at his fiancé for the first time with vulnerability in his eyes.

But Magnusson was looking at Tyler.

"He turned me, so I have a special bond with him, yes. But that's only part of it. He's special to all of us," he said, gesturing at Kelly, Jesse and himself. "To all our kind. He's the oldest. Survived the longest. He gives us all meaning, even if he feels like his own meaning has been lost." He paused and leaned forward before continuing. "If he lives, he can be helped." Magnusson's face shifted. Emotion made his eyes shine. "But if his crimes—justified or not—are what makes the court put execution on the table..." He paused again. Tyler felt like he was about to be sucked into a whirlpool, and the only thing keeping him afloat was the certainty in Magnusson's gaze. "If that happens, not only will that be unbearable on a personal level...but it will set a precedent we can't afford to live with."

"You can't pretend you don't know about all this, Lomax," Kelly said, his voice flat as ice. "It's all over the news. You must have heard of Magister Soroka addressing it?"

Tyler tore his eyes from Magnusson's face, which was echoing his own pain to meet the lawyer's gaze. The levelness of it allowed him to fight enough breath into his lungs to speak. "Dragomir Soroka. Yeah, I've seen him on the telly."

"He is to international haemophile politics what Ivor Novák is to those in the UK."

"Ivor...who?" Tyler blinked. He felt ill. He felt tired. Above all, he was desperate to untangle what all this meant for Lucien but couldn't calm down enough to ask.

"Ivor Novák," Kelly said. "Our parliamentary representative? The one who spearheaded the public awareness campaign after the Blood Winter murders?"

Tyler shook his head. "Okay. Whatever. What do I care about these guys?"

"They are out there fighting to make everything better for people like us, Tyler," Jesse said fervently. "They fight for haemophile rights—for their right to exist without persecution, for their right to live independently like Emory instead of being locked up in compounds, afraid to be part of the world, fighting for their marriage rights, working rights, all of it."

"None of that is my fight," Tyler insisted.

"It should be," Jesse snapped. "You're right in the middle of it."

"I *can't*," Tyler shouted. He balled his fists into his eyes and didn't lower them again until he was sure he could control his voice. "There's not enough of me to put into any of this, Jesse. Don't you get it?" Jesse watched him uncertainly. "Caring for Lucien is the biggest thing I've ever done, and it's almost killed me. There's not enough of me left for anything else. It's not that I don't want to," he added, his voice quiet and shaking. "I just…can't."

"Okay then," Kelly said, sitting forward after a moment of pained silence. "So focus on what you *can* do."

"Which is what?" Tyler said, exhaustion sapping the words of energy.

"Talk to Lucien," Kelly said. "Get him to talk to me."

"I can't get in that place. I've already tried. They won't even admit that it exists."

"Darragh can get you in," Magnusson said.

Tyler blinked at Kelly. "You can?"

He nodded, a hint of a smile curving his lips.

"When?" Tyler breathed.

"As soon as humanly possible," he said, smiling wider. "Pun fully intended."

# Chapter Ten

Tyler didn't sleep that night—or the two nights that followed. He stayed in his flat, his phone close at hand, waiting for it to ring—waiting for Kelly to say it was all arranged, waiting to know if he would see Lucien again.

The days continued to slip away. Tyler ached, body and soul. He ate because he got dizzy when he didn't. He dozed, hoping to meet Lucien in his dreams but woke before sleep fully took him.

News of Lucien's arrest had now made international news. It was trending on social media and was the headline story on every news show. Tyler kept the TV on, day and night, hoping for updates. But there was never anything new.

He stood at the window each day, watching the city bake in the hot summer sun. Apart from the knot of reporters and sightseers that was constantly outside his building, it was like he was frozen in some sort of dream of normalcy. The news kept on rolling. The world kept on going. Emerald stood for and won her election, making a promise to bring more awareness and stability to the sensitive political climate surrounding haemophile rights. She declared her opinion that haemophiles were people, too, and welcome in her city.

To her own vocal surprise and Tyler's, she won by a landslide.

She tried to ring him, but he cut the call every time, wanting the line free. Eventually she gave up. Then, sometime later, the news cycle started to move on. But every moment for Tyler was defined by what wasn't there.

One night he came to himself sprawled on the couch, staring blindly at a live TV report from London. Dragomir Soroka was holding another press conference. His ice-white hair was combed back from his lofty brow. His long-fingered hands clasped the lectern, the glass-like fingernails glinting under the studio lights. The black depths of his eyes, however, seemed to suck all the light in from around him.

Tyler shuddered but made himself turn the volume up.

"...and this is just another example of oppression," he was saying, his cultured voice loud and forceful. "Yes, this individual should be made to answer for his crimes. In the spirit of integration and equality, both human and haemophile must be held accountable for all unlawful or harmful acts. But this *facility* where he is being held? This *court* he will have to face? This goes beyond injustice. It is a crime in itself. And I say again, until we are *heard*, until we are *free*, true justice for our kind cannot be served."

Questions were asked but Tyler didn't hear them. This wasn't about Lucien. This was about Soroka — and politics, and the wider world. The world that had abandoned both of them, left them adrift and apart from each other.

He went to the bathroom to splash water on his face. He stared at himself in the mirror, at the water dripping from the ends of his sandy hair, the hollow look in his eyes.

"Get it together," he muttered, taking a shaking breath. As he let it out, his pulse calmed and he registered that his mobile was ringing.

He yanked it from his pocket and stabbed the answer button. "Kelly?"

"Good evening, Mr. Lomax. We're on."

\* \* \* \*

Tyler still chafed the whole drive down from York, despite the luxury of the car Kelly had arranged. His discomfort grew when they moved into the slow crawl of the London traffic, almost reaching a bursting point when they drove straight past the marble facade of the Old Bailey. The driver took them down a side street then around a corner into what looked like an access alley. The sun was just setting as he climbed out into the stink of hot tarmac and sun-warmed refuse. The car pulled away as soon as he'd closed the door, and he scanned the alley, searching for any sign of life.

"This way, Mr. Lomax."

Tyler started and spun around. Darragh Kelly stood in the shadow of a large gateway behind him. Tyler wiped his palms on his jeans and moved forward on wobbly legs.

The iron gate rolled back as he approached, but Kelly stopped him before he could move inside.

"Apologies," he said, lifting a black hood. "This was the only way they would agree to let you in."

Tyler clenched his teeth over his initial response and nodded. Kelly pulled the hood over his head.

"There are no cameras in the room," Kelly said as he guided Tyler forward with a hand on his arm. "By necessity, it is also heavily locked and soundproofed. A guard can be summoned, but only by pressing the alarm button on the wall. I need to remind you that Lucien is a lot stronger and faster than you. Do you understand the risk?"

"Lucien wouldn't hurt me," Tyler muttered with his voice muffled by the fabric.

Kelly's grip on his arm tightened. "I need you to tell me, out loud, that you understand the risk, Lomax," Kelly said, "or we can't do this."

"I get it," Tyler snapped. "If he wants to kill me, there's nothing anyone can do about it. That's been true ever since I met him. Now, where is he?"

Kelly pushed him on. "You really do care about him, don't you?" he asked after a moment.

"Yes. Is that so hard to believe?"

A pause. "No," Kelly said thoughtfully. "No, it isn't. You'll have to forgive me. I'm constantly surprised by the depth of human feeling." His voice had changed, becoming almost wistful. "I mean that in a good way," he added.

"You're really weird, you know that?" Tyler muttered.

Kelly chuckled. "The law has been my life for hundreds of years. It holds its own beauty, its own special sentience, changing with the world. It's helped me cope with living as long as I have. But I've recently been reminded about what it's like to connect to a living, breathing being. I had thought it was beyond me. Apparently, love is never beyond anyone. Watch this step."

Tyler swallowed his response to negotiate a sudden step down onto hard concrete.

What little light penetrated the hood soon dimmed. The air grew chilly. He shivered. The sounds of locks turning, signals beeping and gates and doors clanking open and shut in front and after him filled his head. Kelly did not speak again. No one else spoke, either.

Finally, Kelly stopped and released his arm.

"Step forward," he said. Tyler obeyed. There was a groan and clank of metal then silence.

Tyler stood stock still, breathing heavily, his throat and mouth dry.

"Tyler?"

Tyler yanked off the hood. He blinked in the low light. He was in a windowless room. The walls, the ceiling and the tiled floor were all black. The only light came from a dim strip bulb on the wall. A bunk with a bare mattress stood against the other.

Tyler barely registered any of this. Lucien stood by the bunk. He was in plain black sweatpants and a T-shirt. No shoes. His feet looked very white against the floor. It was cold enough in the cell for Tyler's skin to ripple with goosebumps, but Lucien showed no visible signs of discomfort. His eyes were locked on Tyler and swam with fire.

Tyler tried to find his voice, but nothing came out. It was like he'd been gutted, boned, stripped of physical feeling and left with nothing but raw emotion.

Lucien took a tentative step closer.

"I can't believe you came."

"Of course I came," Tyler said in a harsh whisper.

Pain flashed in Lucien's eyes. "It would have been easier if you hadn't."

"Easier? How is anything about this easy?"

"You need to live your real life," Lucien said softly.

"I don't want to."

Lucien took in a breath. "It was a dream, Tyler. Eventually, we all have to wake up."

"I never want to wake up."

Tyler closed the distance between them, threaded his hands into Lucien's hair and drew him in. Lucien sighed and opened his mouth to Tyler's searching tongue, running his hands up Tyler's back and digging his fingers into his shoulders.

The smell and feel of Lucien rushed through Tyler like narcotics. He was hard in seconds but found all he wanted was to keep kissing him until he could no longer breathe. Lucien ran his hands down Tyler's arms and looped their fingers together. He broke the kiss to lift Tyler's hands to his mouth and run his lips over his knuckles. Tyler swallowed a groan, his flesh quivering. Lucien's eyes locked on his as he moved from one hand to the other.

"Do you like being touched again?"

"Just by you," Tyler said. "Only you."

Lucien turned Tyler's arm out and planted a series of feathery kisses along the inside of his forearm.

"I never wanted to do this with a human before," he whispered, "not in almost six hundred years of existence. But I've never been able to stop thinking about doing these things with you."

Tyler bit his lip. His cock twitched in his jeans. He longed to shove Lucien onto the bunk, tear his clothing off and bury himself in him so deeply he may never escape again. But watching Lucien float kisses over his skin like he was praying into his flesh was bewitching, setting his blood alight while keeping his body frozen.

Lucien reached his bicep and stepped around Tyler to stand at his back. He trailed his fingers up his bare arms and continued kisses like snowflakes over the back of his neck. Tyler closed his eyes.

"Lucien…"

"Feel it, Tyler," Lucien whispered against his skin as he slowly drew Tyler's T-shirt over his head. "I want you to feel everything I can make you feel, while I still can."

Tyler gasped. "Can we really do this here?"

Lucien didn't answer. Instead, he kissed Tyler's shoulders while snaking his hands around his waist to light a blazing trail over his stomach.

"God, Lucien…"

Lucien pressed himself against Tyler's back. The beginnings of his erection pushing against Tyler's arse made him shiver. But then Lucien blew a slow, hot breath over Tyler's ear and rubbed his fingers over Tyler's nipples.

"Christ," he swore, jerking in his lover's grip. He rested his head back on Lucien's shoulder as he continued to knead and stroke his flesh, pushing his hardening cock against Tyler's arse as he licked and kissed the exposed skin of his neck.

"What if someone comes in?" Tyler managed, knowing full well that if an entire platoon of guards came through the doors with guns drawn, he still wouldn't want it to stop.

"Forget everything else," Lucien murmured against Tyler's jaw and slid a hand toward his waistband. "This moment is just about us."

Tyler just groaned in acknowledgment as Lucien unfastened his jeans and rolled them over his hips. He gasped to feel the cold air playing on the sensitive skin of his hard cock.

"Feel me, Tyler," Lucien whispered, his own voice darkening with arousal as he grasped Tyler's erection.

Tyler let out a low noise, threading his fingers with Lucien's free hand and pressing it against his sternum. He leaned into Lucien, who held him upright as he began to stroke his aching cock. Tyler swore, low and breathy. He kept his eyes closed and sank into the sensation of Lucien's mouth on his shoulder, his body against his back, his hand on his cock, lazily pulling erotic fire through his veins.

Lucien rocked his hips against Tyler's arse, and Tyler's blood sparked.

"Lucien," he growled. "I need you. *Now*."

Lucien tightened his grip on Tyler to stop him moving and ran his tongue over his shoulder to his jaw.

"How do you need me?" he whispered.

"On the bed."

Lucien let out a long, low groan and tightened his grip, almost crushing the breath from Tyler's chest. Then, finally, he let him go. Tyler grabbed him and backed him toward the bunk. Lucien's lips were parted. His eyes were dark and glowing. His erection was visible through his clothing. When they came up against the bunk, Tyler grabbed Lucien's hips and crushed their groins together, capturing his mouth and groaning. Lucien returned the kiss, making low noises, sliding his tongue against Tyler's and kissing him like he would swallow all the moisture in him.

Tyler tugged impatiently at Lucien's clothing until he stripped to the skin. Tyler stepped out of his jeans and gathered Lucien to him again, almost crying to feel his naked body against his own.

The bunk was narrow and hard, but Tyler didn't care. Lucien was louder now, his kisses hot and urgent. Tyler stroked him, sparks flying through his flesh as he thrust against Lucien's most intimate of places.

"I need you, Tyler," Lucien panted against his mouth, threading his hands into Tyler's hair to keep his mouth on his. "I need you inside me. It makes me forget everything else. It's the only thing that does."

Tyler didn't think he'd be able to hang on long enough to prepare Lucien, but when Lucien gasped as Tyler's saliva-lubricated fingers entered him, he quivered with an anticipation stronger than anything he'd ever known.

"Now," Lucien cried. "*Now*, Tyler."

Tyler lined up his cock. He took a deep breath, crushed his own eyes shut, pressed his forehead to Lucien's and slid inside. He made himself go slow. A dark, cold ghost in the back of his mind was telling him to savor it, to remember this forever, that it might be the last time he ever felt this way. But then he was moving deeper. Lucien's body trembled around him and the ghost vanished like fog under the sun.

"Lucien," he growled, tilting his hips so they both lifted from the bunk, and thrust so deep he couldn't tell where he ended and his lover began. "I love you," he said, pulling out, pushing in again. "God, I love you."

Lucien wrapped his legs around Tyler's waist. He gripped his hair and rained kisses on his cheeks, his eyes, his forehead.

"Never stop," he breathed, voice sounding like it was coming from some secret, dark place inside him that hurt him a little. "Never stop feeling like this, Tyler. Promise me."

"I promise," Tyler said, drawing out to the tip and sliding in again, almost sobbing with pleasure. Lucien dug his fingers into Tyler's back. The prick of his fingernails digging into his skin provided a delightful sharp counterpoint to the ecstasy pouring through his body like lava.

Tyler felt like it would last forever — that this was his whole world, the feel, the smell, the sight of Lucien under him, the sensation of being in and surrounded by him. This was all that mattered. This was all that would ever matter.

But the fire kept building. The cyclone swirled faster. Tyler sat up, bringing Lucien with him so he was straddling his lap. Lucien dug his fingers in harder. His mouth opened in a silent scream, and Tyler felt hot stickiness spurt against his belly. Lucien's muscles clamped and catapulted Tyler into climax.

It didn't take long for the cold to penetrate Tyler's flesh. He was laid on his side, propped on one elbow with his hand on Lucien's chest and had to suppress a shiver, but made no move to retrieve his clothes. Lucien lay still and quiet, staring at the ceiling. His skin had returned to its flawless, alabaster perfection, and his eyes were unreadable. Tyler had no idea how long they lay there before he spoke.

"Why did they let you see me?"

Tyler brushed his fingers over Lucien's chest. "The lawyer arranged it. He wants me to get you to talk to him."

"I have nothing to talk to Kelly about."

Tyler stilled his fingers on Lucien's stomach. "He wants to help you."

"I don't need help."

Tyler swallowed. "They might kill you."

"They might," Lucien said. "Unlikely, I would say. That would set a very dangerous example. And this world is the most risk averse I've ever known, despite the risks in it being worse than ever."

Tyler sat up with a growl. "How can you be so cool with all this?"

Lucien propped himself up on his elbows. He looked deep into Tyler's eyes. "We've been through all this. I've hurt people, lots of people. And if they let me out, I would probably hurt more."

"Bad people," Tyler insisted. "You only hurt bad people, people who deserved it."

Lucien smiled. "I think so, yes." His expression fell again. "But there are plenty of individuals out there who hurt people who *don't* deserve it, my kind and yours. Setting an example with me is perhaps the best thing that can happen now. Perhaps it's the last thing I've got left to give the world."

Tyler made a frustrated noise and got up, grabbing his underwear. "You think far too much, you know that?"

"Maybe you don't think enough," Lucien said as Tyler dressed with angry, jerky movements.

"I came here to get you to talk to the lawyer," Tyler said, pulling on a trainer without meeting Lucien's eyes. "So that's what you're going to do."

"No, I'm not."

Tyler stopped dressing. He stared at Lucien, his heart aching. He knelt by the bunk. "Didn't you even think about what this would be like for me?"

Lucien's brow wrinkled. "I'm sorry, Tyler. But what good would talking to Kelly do? I've confessed. They can't let me go."

"He can at least make sure you're treated fairly, right? Isn't that his job?"

Lucien brushed Tyler's hair back from his face. He was smiling sadly. "I'm so glad we got this last bit of time together," he said, resting his hand on Tyler's cheek. "I'll remember it forever. I want you to, too. But now we say goodbye."

"No," Tyler said firmly, clenching his fist. "You don't give up that easily. I won't bloody let you."

Lucien sighed and pulled his clothes back on. Tyler made himself stand back and let him move in silence, resisting the urge to put his hands on him again, gather him close or shake him in frustration.

"This is for the best," Lucien eventually said, sitting on the bunk and holding his hand out for Tyler. Tyler hesitated then allowed Lucien to draw him in to sit next to him. "I was ready to die, Tyler. I thought that was the only viable option left to me. You convinced me otherwise." He ran a knuckle over Tyler's cheek. "You showed me perhaps there is another way. But" — he gestured around the cell — "this is really the only alternative."

"What about the mountains?" Tyler asked quietly. "What about living out there, away from everything? Like we said?"

Lucien bit his lip. The sharp canines against the tender flesh made something ripple through Tyler's skin. "It wouldn't work. Not forever."

"Why not?"

"Forever is such a long time," he whispered. "I know. I've lived it. I would come back—or the world would find me. It always does."

"You could at least try," Tyler insisted. "If you plead not guilty—"

"I can't do that."

Tyler thumped the bunk in frustration. "I hate you sometimes, you know that?"

Lucien put his hand over Tyler's fist. "Whereas I think I love you," he whispered. Tyler stared at him. Lucien gazed into his eyes. "I think I love you, Tyler Lomax. And if I plead not guilty...if I don't take responsibility for the things I've done...what would that do to your love for me?"

"It wouldn't do anything," Tyler said hurriedly. "If it meant you could get out of here, then it wouldn't do anything."

Lucien shook his head. "You're a man of principles. So am I." He lifted Tyler's hand to his mouth and kissed it. "I can't lie."

Tyler swore again and made for the door. He stopped in front of it and turned back. "Are you really stuck here? You really can't get out?"

Lucien was silent. He sat cross-legged on the bunk, staring at his hands.

"You got out of that place of Damon's," Tyler insisted. "You got into my flat. And into the cell at the police station. You could get out of here, too?"

Lucien raised his eyes. "This place is designed to contain haemophiles."

"So was Damon's bunker."

"Damon was an amateur vampire hunter," Lucien said quietly. "A fanatic but ultimately ill-informed.

This place was built by people who knew what they were doing. I can't escape."

"I don't believe you."

Lucien lowered his eyes again. Tyler crouched in front of him and grabbed his hands. "Do it," he whispered. "No lying needed. Just go. Bust out."

"Even if I could, where would I go?"

"Go *home*," Tyler insisted. "Make that mountain castle your home. Stay there. Stay safe."

Lucien's face crumpled. Emotion so raw and red it turned his eyes to liquid glass filled his face. "I told you. I can't, Tyler," he whispered. "The world is too big. Too empty. Too lonely."

"Then I'll go with you," Tyler said suddenly. "Let *me* be this reason for existing you need so much. Let *us*. Wherever you want to go, we'll go together. And I can keep you going. Keep you safe."

Something like hope flared in Lucien's eyes, but it was gone again. "I could never do that to you."

"I want to do it."

Lucien frowned skeptically. "You want to leave everything behind? Your family? Your friends? Your home?"

"I'd have you."

"They'd chase you forever," Lucien said. "If I disappeared, then you disappeared, your kind would hunt for us both."

"That only matters if we get caught."

Lucien stared at him. "You realize that means leaving *everything*, not just people. It means no TV. No phone. No internet. No contact with the outside world."

"I'm so bloody fed up with the outside world," Tyler said vehemently. "All of it. I'd have you, and you'd have me. We could build our own world…together."

Lucien was silent. Tyler squeezed his hands hard. "I can't do that to you, Tyler," he whispered. "You'd hate me for it."

"I wouldn't," Tyler said, shaking his head. "Never."

"You don't understand time like I do," he whispered. "Eventually, you would resent me for all of this. And there would be nowhere to run to. You'd be stuck. And you'd hate me all the time instead of just some of the time. And I couldn't live with that."

"You're wrong," Tyler growled. "You're *so* fucking wrong."

"I won't hurt you."

"You *are* hurting me," he cried. "By letting this happen you're hurting me."

Lucien flinched. His eyes were brimming with pain. He opened his mouth. Tyler froze. But then a loud buzz filled the air, and with a clank, the door opened.

"Time's up," came a gruff, unfamiliar voice and the hood was thrust back over Tyler's head.

"Wait," he called. "Wait! I'm not done."

"I'm afraid you are," the voice continued, and he was manhandled away.

"Lucien," he called, "talk to Kelly. Please. There must be something we can do."

He called Lucien's name again but got no response. The sound of the cell door clanging closed behind him was loud, even over his shouting.

\* \* \* \*

"What do you mean, he said no?"

Kelly spread his hands in a weary gesture. "He won't see me. He's not going to enter a defense. He's not going to trial. He will be extradited to the court in Russia for sentencing at some undisclosed date." Kelly picked up his briefcase and made for the door of Tyler's hotel room. "We tried, Lomax. But I'm all out of ideas. I'm sorry."

Tyler threw a mug at the door after Kelly closed it behind him. It smashed and the shards rained on the blood-red carpet.

Tyler sank onto the strange bed and put his head in his hands. The noise of London was muted behind the soundproof window, but Tyler still felt the roaring in his head, in his chest, in his belly. He thought he might be sick. He closed his eyes and willed his breath to draw in and out.

Finally, he reached for his phone. His hand was shaking as he dialed.

"Tyler?"

Tyler couldn't make himself speak. He breathed, but his chest was shaking with the effort.

"Tyler, are you there?"

"Jesse," Tyler said, voice choked with emotion. "How do you do it?"

A pause. "Do what?"

"Love these bastards," he said, sniffing loudly, swiping angry tears from his eyes. "How do you love one of these ageless, blood-sucking freaks and not go fucking crazy?"

Jesse murmured something to someone out of range of his phone. Tyler heard a door close then Jesse Truelove taking a deep breath.

"It's not easy," he said softly. "But you can't help who you fall for."

"He wouldn't talk to Kelly," Tyler said. "He wouldn't lift a finger to change anything—not for himself, not for me." He blinked at the white ceiling. "What the fuck am I supposed to do now, huh?"

"I guess you come home," Jesse said quietly.

"Then what?"

Another pause. "I dunno, mate," Jesse said quietly. "Emory and I found a way through all the shit. Sorry you guys couldn't."

Tyler swore and threw his arm over his eyes.

"Life's actually at the top of its game when it's putting you through the ringer like this," Jesse said, so quietly Tyler almost didn't hear. "You may not believe it, but this means you actually give a shit. It's a good thing. And, well...seems I owe you an apology for thinking you didn't."

"I'm a dickhead, Jesse," Tyler said wearily. "I already know that. I don't need anyone to tell me."

"You're not a dickhead," Jesse said softly. "A moron, maybe...at least you were. But now?" He sighed noisily. "You're a good man, Tyler. You tried for Lucien. Really tried."

"Fuck-all good it did."

"Look... Why don't you come over when you get back? We can talk this through. No one knows Lucien like Emory does. Perhaps he can help—"

Tyler hung up.

Tyler spent the day wandering aimlessly around London, moving with the crowds, barely registering the buildings, noise or the sweltering heat. Once, he stood outside the Old Bailey until two police officers came along and moved him on. He went back to the hotel, drew the curtains, turned off the lights and lay on the bed in the dark and the silence.

# Chapter Eleven

The hotel room had blackout curtains so Tyler soon lost track of both night and day. He woke from a light sleep some time that must have been late at night because of the utter silence in the hotel around him. His stomach growling was loud in the stillness. He sighed and turned on the bedside light, thinking of searching for the room service menu. The sight of the figure sitting in the chair by his bed made him swear and scramble from the tangle of bedding with his heart thumping against his ribs.

"Calm down, human. I'm not here to hurt you."

Even sat down, Tyler could tell the haemophile must be close to seven feet tall. His face was the color of bone, his hair whiter than his bloodless flesh. His eyes were deep, dark and blacker than a moonless night.

"What the fuck?" was all Tyler could manage.

"I said," the stranger said, voice low and commanding, "calm down." He wrinkled his nose. "Your fear smells like ammonia."

Tyler felt a ripple like ice water go over his skin. He got his breathing under control while glancing nervously at the door.

"You can leave if you want, but then you won't hear what I've got to say."

"You're that big-shot haemo," Tyler breathed. "You're all over the news."

"Magister Dragomir Soroka, at your service." He inclined his head. His eyes never moved from Tyler's face. When he spoke, his long canines glinted against the red of his mouth. "I believe we have a mutual friend."

"We do?"

"The unfortunate soul being detained in an illegal facility beneath the Old Bailey?"

"How do you know Lucien?"

Soroka uncrossed his legs and leaned forward. The light glinted in his eyes making them look like polished onyx. "Lucien is a very well-known figure in our world, a living legend, a breathing ghost from a bygone era. The fact that he is being held captive by humans is unthinkable."

"You're out of the loop, mate," he said. "Lucien *wants* to be in the bloody place."

"I don't believe that."

"Yeah? Go speak to him."

"I intend to…after I've finished speaking to you."

The way Soroka was looking at him made Tyler's flesh crawl on his bones. "How the fuck did you get in here, anyway?"

"I can help Lucien, Mr. Lomax," Soroka said quietly. "And I will—if you do something for me in return."

Tyler narrowed his eyes. "Help him *how*?"

"You…care…for him, don't you?" Soroka said, curling his lip so his fangs were exposed.

"Yes," Tyler said, trying not to stare. "Of course I bloody do — more than he does for me, apparently."

"Oh, he cares for you, too. Believe me. He's just blinded by a long, long life lived by some backward principles instilled in him by a dead god from the dark ages. And you should know that whatever Magnusson has told you, many of my kind would be glad to see him quietly taken away. He's too unpredictable...too dangerous." Soroka flicked a finger in dismissal. "He doesn't fit in with my kind's current plan for integration. But we can't just imprison someone, or worse, just because they are *inconvenient*."

"He thinks otherwise."

Soroka stared at him, long and hard. "I believe I can make him see differently. But you have to agree to something first."

Tyler frowned. "What?"

Soroka stood. Tyler fought the urge to step back. The haemophile towered over him as he moved closer.

"You have to agree to keep away from him, Mr. Lomax."

Tyler blinked. "What?"

"If Lucien is freed, you have to agree to stay away from him. Even if he comes to you... Even if he begs you to see him, you must decline. Do you understand?"

"Why the hell should I do that?"

"Because it's in his best interests...and yours."

"Our interests?" Tyler bristled, squaring his shoulders. "I love him — and he loves me."

Soroka's eyes flared. "Our war is being fought on many fronts, Mr. Lomax. Ivor Novák fights for us in the UK parliament. Darragh Kelly fights for us in the courts of law. Baron Emory von Magnusson fights for us within the hearts and communities of the human population. We need these haemophiles doing what they do, all of them. But we also need me."

"And what do *you* do?"

In a movement too quick to see, he'd grabbed Tyler by the throat and slammed him against the wall. Tyler's breath rushed out of him. He gasped, scrabbling at the hand on his throat, but the haemophile's grip was like iron.

"I'm the one who's not afraid to draw blood," he whispered. "My kind needs a champion, one that isn't afraid to do what's needed, no matter how ugly. The hunters and the hate groups are gaining power, growing in numbers. Kidnapping and torture is just the start. What might they be bold enough to do next?"

"I'm not with them," Tyler rasped, clawing at the grip on his throat.

"I will get Lucien out of that place. And you" — Soroka squeezed tighter. Tyler's eyes bulged in his head — "are to *stay away* from him. Understand?"

The grip vanished. Tyler crumpled to the floor, gasping and coughing. He pulled air into his burning lungs, clutching at his throat. His hand came away bloody. He got to his feet on shaking legs and blinked around the room. It was empty.

He might have believed it was a nightmare, if it weren't for the bruises on his neck the next morning. He got the first train back to York then went straight to his flat and locked himself in. He thought about calling Emerald, then Jesse. He even thought about calling DI Walker.

But what would he say? The vampire rights activist off the telly had appeared in his hotel room and threatened his life?

He lay on the sofa, rubbing his neck, frowning and trying to figure out what the hell was going on. He searched the internet for everything he could find about Soroka. He was vocal about his views and an impassioned speaker. But nothing Tyler found explained what had happened. He went to his bedroom, shut the door and the curtains, climbed into bed and pulled the duvet over his head.

The adrenaline crashed out of him in a wave. He shuddered. He cried. Then, finally, he fell asleep.

What woke him was a cool touch on his forehead. It soothed his troubled dreams and eased the tension in his limbs. He blinked his eyes open.

He could hear rain lashing the windows. Lightning flickered in the gaps between his curtains. Thunder rolled in the distance. The storm had finally broken. The air felt alive, like it was finally breathing again.

But that only registered on the very edges of Tyler's consciousness. He recognized the touch of the hand on his skin, the feel of the rain-damp hair brushing his chest, the smell of dark wine and autumn leaves that filled his nose.

"Lucien," he breathed, reaching blindly into the dark, pulling him close.

The kiss was slow but urgent. Tyler sobbed, running his hands all over Lucien's body, trying to believe he was really there.

"I'm here," Lucien breathed. "I'm here, Tyler."

They made love slowly and passionately with the storm roaring beyond the windows. They didn't speak but breathed their pleasure into each other's ears without words, drawing it out as long as possible. Lightning lit up the room, the wave crashed and Tyler came.

They lay tangled in Tyler's sheets with cool air playing on their skin. Tyler lay very still, breathing in the smell of Lucien's hair as he lay with his head on

Tyler's chest, listening to the thunder and rain sweeping over the city.

"I don't understand," he finally made himself say, knowing it would burst the bubble but unable to stay silent any longer.

"I changed my mind."

"Which part of your mind?"

Lucien shifted his weight onto one elbow and ran the pads of his fingers over Tyler's face. "I want to go, Tyler," he murmured softly. "But I don't want to go on my own."

Tyler swallowed. "You said it wouldn't work."

Lucien didn't speak.

"What happened, Lucien?"

"That doesn't matter now."

"Yes, it does," Tyler said, reaching for the bedside lamp.

"No," Lucien said, grabbing his wrist. "Can we just stay in the dark together a few moments more?"

"Why?"

"Because the minute you turn the light on, you're going to have to tell me who did that to your neck and everything will change."

Tyler's chest constricted. "He got you out, didn't he? Soroka?"

Lucien was still for a long time. Then he let out a long sigh and switched on the light. His eyes were bright with some unknown emotion. His jaw was tight. He was naked and beautiful, and all Tyler wanted to do was kiss him, but the tension in his body now was too palpable to ignore.

Lucien ran his fingers over Tyler's neck with a line between his eyebrows.

"He made me realize it's not just about me…or us." He raised his eyes. "He told me to go immediately… alone. But I had to see you."

"He told me to stay away from you," Tyler said softly. "He told me if he got you out that I had to leave you alone."

Lucien's face flattened. "Do you want to?"

"No," Tyler said urgently, grabbing his wrist and kissing his mouth. "No, no, *no*. I can't stay away from you, Lucien. I *won't* stay away. No one can make me."

Lucien grabbed Tyler's face and kissed it all over. "I can't stay away, either," he breathed. "I love you and I can't live out there without you, without my new reason for being alive." He stopped and looked hard into Tyler's eyes. "But we need to leave tonight."

Tyler blinked. "Tonight?"

Lucien nodded. "Did you mean what you said? Will you leave it all behind? Think, Tyler. You have to think carefully. Now more than ever, if you come, you can't ever come back."

"I don't care about anything but you," Tyler insisted. "We'll go together. Right now."

Lucien bit his lip, weighing him up for a painful timeless moment. Then he nodded and stood. "Get dressed. We have to be quick."

"They won't catch you," Tyler said, getting out of bed and dressing. "You move faster than any human, right?"

"It's not humans I'm worried about," Lucien said quietly as he pulled on his shirt.

Tyler went still. Something in Lucien's tone made his blood run cold.

"Lucien…what aren't you telling me?"

Lucien didn't answer. He just continued dressing without meeting Tyler's eyes.

"Lucien..." Tyler took his shoulders and made him look in his eyes. "I'm not scared of Soroka, any more than I'm scared of Damon or his friends, or of the police, or of leaving everything behind to be with you."

"Are you sure about that, Tyler?"

He took Lucien's hand. "I'm not scared, Lucien. I never have been."

Lucien smiled. He pressed a soft kiss to Tyler's cheek then wrapped his arms around his neck, nuzzling Tyler's hair. "I believe you, Tyler. Now grab what you need... *now*."

Tyler threw some clothes into a bag while Lucien waited in the hall. He hovered in his living room for a minute, looking around, knowing he may not see his flat or his city ever again. When he looked inside himself, however, he found all he was feeling was excitement.

"Tyler?"

"One quick call," Tyler said and found his phone where he'd left it next to the sofa.

"Tyler." Emerald's voice was croaky, like she'd just woken, but still hard with anger. "For the record, I will be kicking your arse six ways to Sunday for disappearing on me again. But first I just need you to tell me you're okay?"

"I'm more than okay, Emmy." Tyler smiled. "I'm the best I've been in years."

"Are you high or something?" Emerald asked after a heartbeat.

"Sober as a judge. But listen. I don't have much time."

Lucien had come to the door and was holding out his hand.

"Tyler?" Emerald sounded strained. "What's going on?"

"You need to know I'm happy, Emmy," Tyler said. "I'm happy, at last. But I'm going away for a while."

"What? Why?"

"You're the one who said I should get out of town," Tyler said, moving toward Lucien. "See more of the world. Guess I've just finally realized that was good advice. I just wanted to tell you that I love you before I left."

"Tyler, you're scaring me now."

"Nothing to be scared of," Tyler said as he took Lucien's hand. "Not nothing. Not ever again."

She sighed noisily. "If you say so. I love you, too, just so you know. Promise me you'll stay safe."

"I promise." He hung up.

Lucien kissed him. "Ready?"

Tyler smiled and nodded. "I was born ready."

Lucien grinned. It lit his face and eyes and made him look startlingly young. "Then let's go. You'll have to leave that," he said, nodding at the phone.

Tyler went to place it on the sofa. A picture pinged in, with a message from Jesse.

*Tyler. Ring me. Now.*

Tyler frowned. It was a screenshot of a news article.

*Prominent Haemophile Solicitor Darragh Kelly Found Dead. Human Hate Group Suspected. Manhunt Launched...*

Tyler couldn't move. His belly filled with jagged glass. Jesse was ringing him.

"Tyler?" Lucien stood near the door with a concerned frown. "Has something happened?"

Tyler took a few breaths to steady himself. Then he raised his head, smiled, turned the phone off and threw it on the sofa. He went to Lucien and kissed him.

"Nothing to do with us," he whispered. "Let's go. The world is waiting."

## Blood and Bonds:
## Hunt in the Night
### S. J. Coles

## Coming August 2024

### *Excerpt*

Mason knew it was over when Amelia got out of bed and started dressing in silence. Rain lashed the bedroom windows. Thunder rolled and cracked in the night beyond the half-drawn blinds. The storm had been a long time coming and was a blissful relief from the heatwave that had been choking the city of York for weeks. But all Mason registered was the stiffness in Amelia's movements as she buttoned her blouse.

She never stayed the night. By mutual agreement this—whatever *this* was—was just about what time they could snatch around their cases. But she usually stayed for a while after the sex…to talk. She liked to talk. Mason had come to like it, too.

But now she stared fixedly ahead as she dressed, and the silence was heavy between them.

"Everything okay?"

She sighed. "I think it's time."

He knew what was coming but, somehow, Mason just felt…blank. "Time for what?"

Amelia sat on the edge of the bed to pull her heels on. "Come on, Mason. We both know this has run its course."

Mason searched for the right reaction. "I thought we were having fun."

"We were. We did. But there's something missing, isn't there?"

He didn't meet her eye.

"Mason, if you can't be honest with me, at least be honest with yourself."

"Honest about what?"

"You need...more. I don't know what, but you're not getting it from me."

"That's not true."

"It is," she said with a frank look. "I'm okay with that. But I'm not okay with sex that isn't blowing both our minds. Life's too short."

He blinked. "You've never complained."

"It's not a complaint," she said and retrieved her earrings from the dressing table, "or a comment on your performance." The smile she gave herself in the mirror eased his wounded pride. "But I know you're not getting everything *you* want."

"I like you, Amelia. I thought you liked me."

"I do. And this has been good. But it's time to end it."

"Is this because of that email from HR? About relationships at work?"

"This isn't a relationship," she said, patting his leg. "We were both agreed on that from the start. And, yes, technically, I am your boss —"

"Boss's boss," he said with the lop-sided smile that usually brought an answering smile from her.

But her lips remained a flat line. "Do yourself a favor, Mason. Open yourself up. You don't limit yourself at work. Don't do it in your personal life."

"I wasn't aware I was."

She looked at him hard. "It's time for something new…for both of us. That's it." She kissed him softly and straightened. "You understand, right?"

Mason opened his mouth to answer before he knew what the answer would be. His phone started buzzing on the bedside table. Amelia's rang half a heartbeat later.

"It's the station," Amelia said as she frowned at her phone screen.

"Me, too," Mason said. "That can't be good."

\* \* \* \*

Mason crawled along the country roads, hardly able to see ten feet in front of the rain-pelted windscreen.

He cursed under his breath the whole, fraught journey then out loud as he climbed out into a lay-by crowded with police cars and SOCO vans. A uniformed constable appeared with an umbrella, which promptly turned inside out, dousing them both with spray.

"Don't bother," Mason said, raising his voice over the wind. "Where is he?"

"This way, DI Walker."

Mason bent his head to follow the constable's bright yellow rain poncho through an open gate. They battled uphill through the wind with his shoes sinking into four inches of mud.

Finally they came under the relative shelter of some close-growing trees. Mason stepped, blinking, into the brightly lit interior of a forensic tent.

"Lovely night for a murder." A petite woman with close-cropped orange hair appeared at his side in a white forensic bodysuit. She was bearing a cup of take-out coffee and a grim expression.

"You're telling me," Mason muttered, sipping the coffee and examining the organized chaos around him. "So, Vickers, who found him?"

"A uniform did, out here doing a routine sweep. The victim's partner rang the station a few hours ago. He's been gone less than twenty-four hours, but the partner was pretty insistent."

"Has next of kin been informed?"

"Not yet. He fits the description of the missing person all right, but there's no ID."

"And just how much evidence have we lost?" Mason said as the wind renewed its efforts to tear the tent from the ground.

Vickers winced. "They won't know for sure until they get him back to the lab," she said, heading to the plastic curtain that protected the crime scene. "But doc says there's unlikely to be any fingerprints or DNA."

Mason swallowed a curse. "And how long does she reckon he's been out here?"

"She's not sure about that, either."

Mason frowned as a scene tech took his barely touched coffee and handed him his own suit and gloves. "I've never known Kumar to not have an estimated Time of Death."

"Yeah, well, this is kinda beyond her expertise. Didn't they tell you on the phone?"

Mason's heart sank. "Tell me what?"

"The victim's a haemophile."

His stomach dipped. "Who?"

"We think...Darragh Kelly," Vickers said, holding back the plastic curtain.

Mason stared at his DC for a long moment then took a breath, pulled on his mask and stepped through the curtain.

Mason had seen many bodies over the course of his career. He remembered his first murder victim like it was yesterday. He'd been a drug dealer, beaten to death by a rival while they'd both been high. They'd caught the perpetrator within twenty-four hours. He'd walked into an A&E with two broken hands and blood on his clothes that wasn't his. It was an open and shut case, and neither of the men had been good people. But seeing the victim's body in the dumpster, thrown away like trash, had been a shard of ice driven into the pit of Mason's stomach.

He'd had that same feeling to a greater or lesser extent with every body he'd examined since.

But this was different. The feeling was deeper. Colder. More like fear.

The haemophile lay in a shallow, muddy hole between the roots of a tree. One leg was bent under him. His arms were splayed. The techs had removed as much soil as possible, but the dirt clung to his fine suit and the luminous blue of his disarranged tie. His shirt had probably been a very crisp white. Now it was filthy and clung to the pale skin like cling film. The eyes were open and hooded. Even from where he stood, Mason could see they were green, like ivy or bottle glass — and eerily bright, even in death. He made himself step closer.

The victim's hair was red — not the bright orange-red of Vickers' natural ginger, but blood-red. Not dyed, but not human, either.

Mason examined the single, neat hole in the center of the forehead with an uncomfortable feeling.

"I tell you what, Walker," Dr. Kumar said, standing from her kneeling position next to the body. Her face was obscured by a mask, but her eyes behind her goggles were dark with mixed feelings. "Haemophile forensics are baffling. I'm not sure I can face the amount of stuff I'm going to have to un-learn to be able to deal with this."

"I hear you, doc. Just give me what you do have."

The doctor gazed down at the body with an expression that was part-regretful, part-bemused. "I'm guessing gunshot to the head as cause of death. It looks like it was pretty close range. But their bones don't break the same way ours do, so I can't be sure."

"Any bullet?"

"There's an exit wound," Kumar said, nodding to the head. "But the techs haven't found anything."

"So probably killed elsewhere."

Kumar shrugged again, unwilling to commit.

"Anything else?"

"Time of death…I don't know. I'll have to do some reading on decomp and body temp statistics in haemophiles—if there's even any reading to be found. Oh…and I think both arms are broken," she said, pointing. "The humerus on both left and right appear misaligned. I'll know more once I've done x-rays."

"That must have taken a hell of a lot of strength," Vickers murmured. "Their bones are like iron, aren't they?"

Kumar nodded. "That much I do know. But that's about it. No ID on the body, either, so we can't even be sure—"

"It's Darragh Kelly, all right," Mason said. "I met him once."

"Shit," Vickers muttered. ""As if we didn't have enough mess with the whole Lucien-escape thing. Oh," she winced. "Sorry, boss."

Mason shook his head. "No, you're right. That is very much my personal mess. But let's just deal with one earth-shatteringly unorthodox crime at a time."

"Seconded," Kumar said, shaking her head.

"He was dumped," Mason murmured, pacing around the scene. "In a shallow grave. Hasty. Undignified. Not meant to be found?"

"There's no regret here," Vickers mused. "But no passion, either. The execution-style killing, the impersonal dump site… It's almost…"

"Routine," Mason finished for her.

"Right," Vickers nodded. "Even though there's absolutely nothing else routine about it."

"Also right," Mason said. "Okay," he said, finally looking away. "I want a full work up—forensics and autopsy, everything you have on the scene and the body. Whatever there is, I want it."

"You'll have it," Kumar said levelly. "If it's here, you'll have it."

Mason nodded. "Vickers, you're with me."

She nodded and followed him back through the curtain. "Next of kin?"

"I'm afraid so."

Vickers sighed as they stripped out of the white suits. "This part never gets any easier. Aw *crap*," she added as she checked her phone.

"What?"

She held out the phone. "This has already hit the internet."

Mason swore. "How?"

"The partner, Tom Addams? He posted online trying to find Kelly. The news sites have taken a wild guess and run with it. The story's everywhere. And this time the bastards are actually right."

"This does not help us...or Addams," Mason muttered as he stepped into the howling rain.

"I doubt he's thinking straight, boss," Vickers muttered. "Poor guy's been in limbo all day."

Mason suppressed a surge of guilt. "Well, let's go put him out of his misery."

"And into a worse one," Vickers murmured with a solemn expression.

\* \* \* \*

Tom Addams was a pleasant-faced young man, classically handsome with a chiseled jaw, tanned skin and chestnut curls that seemed to effortlessly fall into place. Mason spent a full fifteen minutes in the bathroom mirror every morning attempting to tame his unruly ash-brown waves with product and, even given the circumstances, knew a small stab of jealousy. But he did not envy the way his news leached the color from the man's face.

"I'm so sorry," Mason said softly, knowing how inadequate the words were, but knowing there was nothing else he could do except say them.

Addams sank into a chair and put his head in his hands. Vickers went to see if she could find some water.

They were in one of the many private sitting-rooms in Oswald House, Baron Emory Von Magnusson's luxurious mansion. The furniture and décor were minimal but opulent, and the soundproof glass reduced the clamor of the weather to a dim rumble. The air was laced with the scent of the flowers on the coffee table but was thick with the intensity of the security engineer's sorrow.

Vickers returned with a glass of water. Addams took it with a shaking hand but didn't drink.

"Mr. Addams, I'm sorry. I know this is a terrible time, but would you be up to answering a few questions?"

Addams continued to stare into space, ashen-faced.

"We can come back tomorrow," Vickers started, but Addams shook his head.

"No," he said, gulping water. He coughed and set the water aside. "No, I want this over with. I want whoever did this to be found." He raised his eyes to Mason. They were dry but red and deep as wells. "Whatever you need. Ask me."

Mason took a seat. Vickers remained standing and withdrew a notepad and pen from her pocket.

"First, I have to ask if Mr. Kelly had any enemies?"

Addams's mouth turned down at the corners. "Enemies? Darragh? How long a list do you want?"

Mason winced internally. "He was involved in some…controversial politics?"

"Putting it mildly," Addams said bitterly. "Arranging the first legal adoption of a human child by a haemophile? Fire-fighting Lucien's vigilante attacks? Not to mention his work on the haemo-human marriage bill…" Addams swallowed and went silent.

"Was there anyone in particular that objected?"

"People have protested at the gates, thrown stones, vandalized the place. They picketed the courthouse on the night of the Baron's hearing…"

Mason nodded. "I remember. That must have been hard."

A shaky smile warmed Addams' face. "But it was all for love, DI Walker. Everything Darragh did…" He took a shaking breath. "He wasn't an easy person to get close to. People who knew him, even other haemophiles, thought him cold...stiff. He gave the impression that the law was his life, his only passion. But he knew love. He knew it deeply." He took a shaking breath. "He fought for love in the only way he knew how...through the law. He didn't deserve this."

"Mr. Addams,"

"Tom," the young man interrupted, closing his eyes. "Please. Call me Tom."

"Of course," Mason said, "Tom. You are right. Darragh did not deserve this. But you are also right in that not everyone saw his work the way you do. I know it's hard, but are there any individuals that you know of that were more...persistent than the others? Anyone who threatened him directly?"

Tom picked at his fingernails. He had stopped shaking, but the color still hadn't returned to his face. Mason wondered if it ever would. "The hate mail has increased a lot recently. The marriage legislation is being finalized as we speak." He raised his eyes. A sad smile turned up his mouth. "Emory and Jesse's wedding is booked for October Thirty-First. Halloween night. Some people are saying it's inappropriate... We're all trying so hard to move away from the concept of vampires. But Darragh insisted that getting married the very day the law becomes live sends a strong message." Tom sighed noisily. "To answer your question, DI Walker—"

"Mason," Mason said with a half-smile.

He was rewarded with a weak one in return. "Mason," Tom said softly. "To answer your question...no. There are so many people out there that hate us...that hate *him*...I couldn't pick any one of them that hates more than the others."

Mason exchanged glances with Vickers. Her face reflected the grimness he felt inside.

"Let's focus on his most recent movements, then. When was the last time you spoke to him?"

"Last night," Tom said. "He was in London this last week, working with Honor McLeary."

"She's Ivor Novák legal assistant, isn't she?"

Tom nodded. "Novák is the official parliamentary representative for Haemophile Affairs, the public face and voice of the movement. But Honor is the one who's been doing all the legwork, with the legal stuff, anyway." Another shaky smile. "I must confess, I'm only a security engineer. I don't understand a whole lot about Darragh's legal world."

"I'm willing to bet you understand more than you think you do," Mason said softly. "So, he was in London?"

Tom nodded. "He was traveling back last night. He rang me from the car, told me to go to bed and he'd see me tonight." He gave an awkward shrug. "Dating a haemophile is sort of a nocturnal activity. So yeah, I took the chance to get some sleep. But when I woke up, there was this text from his number on my phone. I knew straight away something was wrong."

His hands were shaking again as he pulled out his phone and tapped the screen. He held out it.

The text message had been sent at four-sixteen that morning.

*Sorry, dearest. Something's come up. Urgent. Will be unreachable for a few nights but don't worry. I'll be back soon. Love you.*

"Was this unusual for him?" Mason said, watching Tom's face carefully.

Tom shook his head. "No. His schedule's pretty hectic. And when we're apart, our sleeping patterns are all over the place. We don't often get a chance even for phone calls."

"So what made you think something was wrong?"

"He doesn't call me 'dearest'…ever." Tom's face was hard. "He calls me *acushla*. It's Gaelic for —"

"Darling," Vickers put in with a crooked smile. "My Nanna's from Cork. She used to call me that when I was small."

Tom nodded, his eyes bright with unshed tears. "Literally it means 'pulse' or 'vein'…something from the heart. From a haemophile it had even more meaning." He closed his eyes.

"Tom, if you want —"

Tom shook his head, sipped the water again and set it aside, slowly and deliberately. "No. No, I want to continue." Tom met Mason's eyes then Vickers'. "Darragh did not send me that text. Or if he did, he was telling me something was wrong."

"Sixteen minutes past four…" Mason looked at Vickers. "That's before sunrise."

Vickers nodded.

"What happened to him?" Tom asked shakily. "Am I allowed to know?"

Mason tapped his fingertips together but didn't break eye contact. "If you think it would help?"

Tom bit his lip. "During Blood Winter, another haemophile was killed. Terje Kristiansen. Died of blood loss after being shot."

Mason nodded, keeping his face blank. "I remember."

"I know Terje," Tom said. "He visits Oswald House. After he died…he came back." Tom gripped the arms of his chair. "Unless you tell me how Darragh died, I don't think I'll be able to believe it."

Mason remembered the broken body, filthy and cold — the staring eyes, the unnatural stillness.

"He was shot, Tom," Mason said softly. "Shot in the head."

Tom's eyes darkened. "So he's dead. Really dead."

Mason felt Vickers' eyes on him. He opened his mouth to speak when the door opened.

"Tom?" A young man stood in the doorway. Dark, uneven hair fell in his face. He had facial piercings and tattoos on his arms. His striking face was a mask of horror as he took in Mason and Vickers, then it clouded with anger.

"Tom, my God," he hurried forward and sat next to him. "They shouldn't be talking to you *now*." He put his arms around Tom. "Oh God. Oh God, Tom. I'm sorry. I'm *so* sorry."

Tom held on tight, so tight his grip must have been hurting, but the two men just held each other and rocked as silent sobs shook Tom's body.

"Jesse," he sobbed. "He's gone. He's really gone."

The newcomer directed a glare at Mason. "What the fuck do you think you're doing, huh? Interrogating him when he's just found out his partner's been murdered?"

"Mr. Truelove?" Mason guessed.

"It doesn't matter who I am," Jesse Truelove retorted. "Get out...*now*."

"No," Tom choked, straightened and rubbing at his blotchy face. "No, Jesse. I want to talk to them. I have to feel like I'm doing something."

"You've done enough for tonight, mate," Truelove replied, wiping at Tom's face so tenderly that Mason felt he should look away. "You need to rest. Cry. Scream. Anything. But being rational and answering questions?" He shook his head. "There's time for that tomorrow."

"Actually," Mason said, "I think we have all we need for now. Vickers?"

Vickers nodded and made for the door. Mason paused before leaving.

"Mr. Truelove?"

"What?" Jesse's face was pale with emotion.

"Look after him, will you?" Mason said quietly. "It's only just sinking in."

Truelove's face softened, and he nodded. "I will. And anything else you need, you call me. Got it?"

Mason nodded. "Got it."

Mason shut the door behind him. Vickers was standing in the lobby, rigid and staring at a figure approaching across the marble floor. Mason's stomach dropped as Baron Emory Von Magnusson joined them.

Mason had seen news footage of the Baron. He'd studied everything to do with him during the endless briefings on his custody case and protests, as well as Lucien's attacks earlier in the summer.

But he hadn't yet met him.

He was larger than Mason could even have imagined. Mason was tall, pushing six-four, and went to the gym whenever his schedule would allow it. He was far from being a reed, but Magnusson dwarfed him. He had to look up to meet his eyes and the suit he wore had to have been custom made to contain those broad, sloping shoulders.

"DI Walker, I believe?" His voice was low and deep as the thunder outside and was weighted with about the same amount of danger.

"Yes, sir," Mason said, dredging some dignity from somewhere. "And this is DC Phoebe Vickers. I'm afraid we have some bad news about Darragh Kelly."

For less than a second, emotion tightened the Baron's passive face. Mason had a hard time maintaining eye contact. But it was gone as quickly as it came.

"Yes, Jesse told me. The police station just rang the house."

"I'm sorry you had to find out that way. Some of this has appeared to have leaked online, and the legal team will be getting ahead…"

"I'd rather know sooner than later." Magnusson glanced at the door. "Jesse's in with Tom?"

Vickers nodded. "He's looking after him. I think he needs it."

Magnusson looked at Mason. "Do you have any idea who has done this dreadful thing?"

"Do you have any suspicions?" Mason asked.

"Tom didn't?" Magnusson said carefully.

"He says there's been widespread hate in response to a lot of Mr. Kelly's work," Mason said in a measured tone. "He wasn't aware of anything more…personal."

"Was this personal?"

Mason weighed his words before speaking. "I don't know yet. Possibly not. But choosing to end someone's life has personal implications, even if they're not conscious."

Magnusson sighed deeply, his large chest swelling.

"I'm afraid I'm no wiser than Tom is. I can tell you about all the targeted attacks we've been subject to, though we have already reported everything."

"Yes and we have those records, thank you," Mason said. "I'll be working my way through those as a first order of priority. But, Baron, just one thing…."

"Yes?"

Mason hesitated. "Could this have been Lucien?"

"Absolutely not."

"You seem very sure of that."

Magnusson was silent for a moment. "Darragh has been managing the fallout from Lucien's behavior for decades. He's very skilled at it. Lucien knows that. They were far from close, but they were not enemies. And Lucien has never once killed without justification."

"Justification alters rapidly, depending on your point of view."

"I understand you have to ask these questions," the Baron eventually replied. "And all I can do is give my word that Lucien did not do this. For one thing, there really was no motive, no matter what you think. For another, I can tell you that Lucien was still incarcerated in London until sunset tonight. I believe Tom was convinced something was wrong from the early hours of this morning."

"Forgive me, Baron, but Lucien got out tonight. He could have got out last night."

Magnusson tilted his head. "How much do you know about haemophiles, DI Walker?"

"A lot more than I did before Lucien blew into town."

Magnusson studied him. Mason realized with a start that he didn't seem to blink. "Then perhaps you've come across the fact that a haemophile can sense their maker, roughly where they are, what they're feeling, however far apart they might be?"

Mason glanced at Vickers, who nodded. "It's true, boss. There are studies being done on it."

"Okay," Mason said carefully. "And Lucien is your maker, so you know where he was last night. How about now?"

A tilting smile curved the Baron's lips. "Nice try, DI Walker. All I can tell you is that he's left the country."

Mason schooled his face. "You just said you could 'sense' him, wherever he was."

"I can. Though the details become harder the greater the distance. I can tell you that he was in London, in his cell, last night and all of today. After sunset, he came to York. Now, he's gone."

Mason started. "He came to York? Why?"

"I'm assuming to fetch Mr. Lomax."

Mason swore under his breath. "So *both* Lucien and Tyler Lomax are gone?"

"I believe so."

Mason ran a hand through his hair, then took a breath. "Thank you, Baron. I apologize for having to ask all this. But there's a lot of unprecedented violence happened in my city, and I can't help but wonder if it's all linked."

"That's because you're good at your job," the Baron. "And I am guessing that Darragh's work will be at the root of all this. But all I can tell you for sure is that Lucien didn't kill him. Now, if you'll excuse me," he stepped to the side. "My family needs me."

# About the Author

S. J. Coles is a Romance writer originally from Shropshire, UK. She has been writing stories for as long as she has been able to read them. Her biggest passion is exploring narratives through character relationships.

She finds writing LGBT/paranormal romance provides many unique and fulfilling opportunities to explore many (often neglected or under-represented) aspects of human experience, expectation, emotion and sexuality.

Among her biggest influences are LGBT Romance authors K J Charles and Josh Lanyon and Vampire Chronicles author Anne Rice.

S. J. Coles loves to hear from readers. You can find her contact information, website details and author profile page at https://www.firstforromance.com/

PUBLISHING

Sign up for our newsletter and find out about all our romance book releases, eBook sales and promotions, sneak peeks and FREE romance books!